STAR WARS®

EPISODE V
THE EMPIRE STRIKES BACK™

VOLUME TWO

Script
ARCHIE GOODWIN

Art
AL WILLIAMSON

Art Assist
CARLOS GARZÓN

Colors
JAMES SINCLAIR

Lettering
RICK VEITCH

DARK
HORSE
COMICS

Spotlight

VISIT US AT
www.abdopublishing.com

Reinforced library bound edition published in 2010 by Spotlight, a division of the ABDO Group, 8000 West 78th Street, Edina, Minnesota 55439. Spotlight produces high-quality reinforced library bound editions for schools and libraries. Published by agreement with Dark Horse Comics, Inc., and Lucasfilm Ltd.

Printed in the United States of America, Melrose Park, Illinois.
092009
012010
♲ PRINTED ON RECYCLED PAPER

Library of Congress Cataloging-in-Publication Data

Goodwin, Archie.
  Episode V : the empire strikes back / based on the Screenplay by
George Lucas ; script Adaptation Archie Goodwin ; artists Al
Williamson & Carlos Garzon ; colorist James Sinclair ; letterer Rick
Veitch. -- Reinforced library bound ed.
     p. cm. -- (Star Wars)
  "Dark Horse Comics."
  ISBN 978-1-59961-701-5 (vol. 1) -- ISBN 978-1-59961-702-2 (vol. 2)
-- ISBN 978-1-59961-703-9 (vol. 3) -- ISBN 978-1-59961-704-6 (vol. 4)
  1. Graphic novels. [1. Graphic novels.] I. Lucas, George, 1944- II.
Williamson, Al, 1931- III. Garzon, Carlos. IV. Empire strikes back
(Motion Picture) V. Title. VI. Title: Episode five. VII. Title: Empire
strikes back.
  PZ7.7.G656Epi 2010
  [Fic]--dc22
                                       2009030860

All Spotlight books have reinforced library bindings and
are manufactured in the United States of America.

Episode V

THE EMPIRE STRIKES BACK

Volume 2

Since the destruction of the Death Star, the Empire has redoubled its effort to crush the growing Rebellion.

Struggling to keep the Rebellion alive, Princess Leia has set up a new base of operations on the ice planet Hoth, where freedom fighters have already met with dangerous ice monsters.

Now detected by an Imperial probe droid sent by Darth Vader, the Rebels prepare to fight just as the first of the Empire's strike force arrives: six Imperial Star Destroyers in the sky, and Imperial Walkers on the ground!

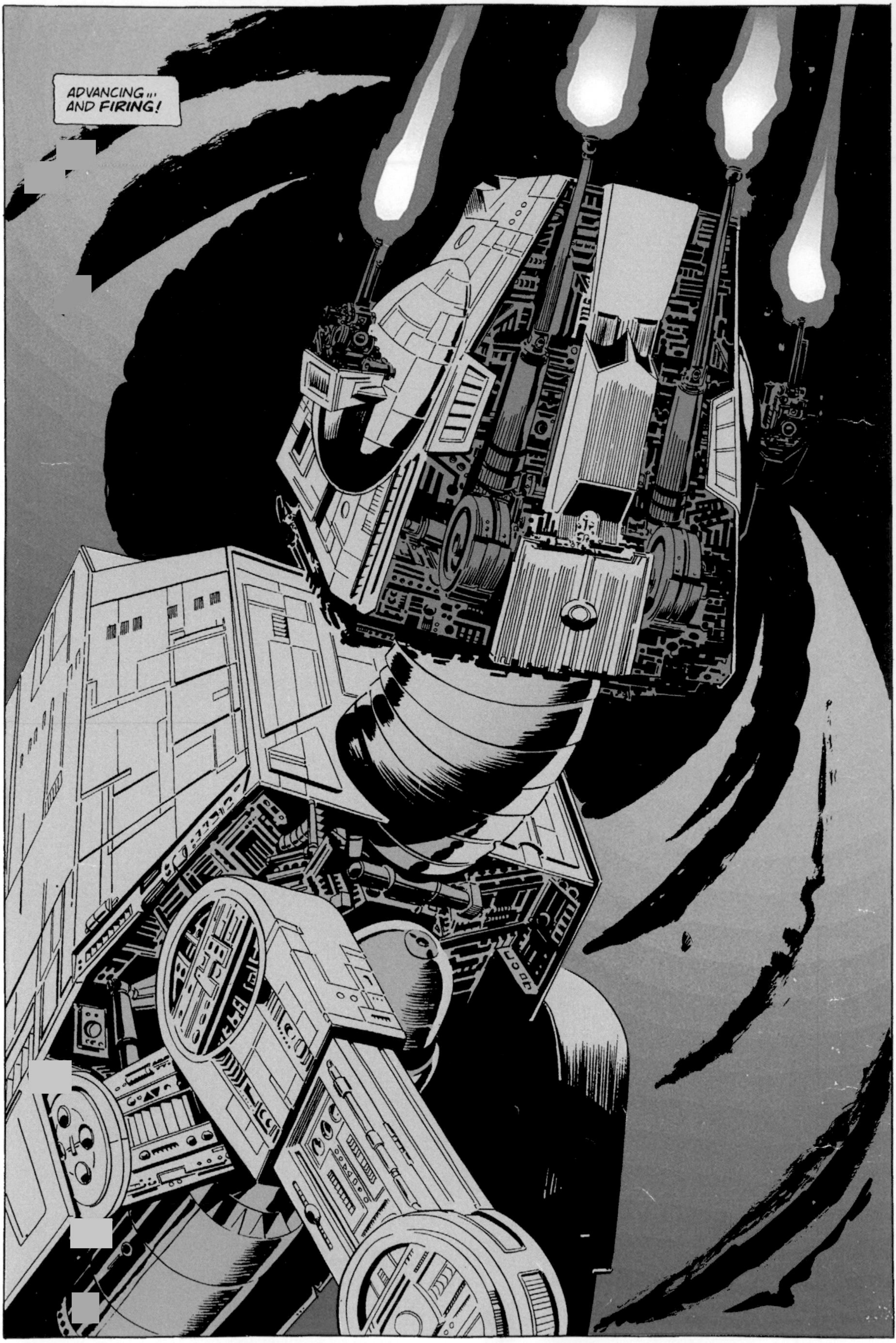
ADVANCING... AND FIRING!

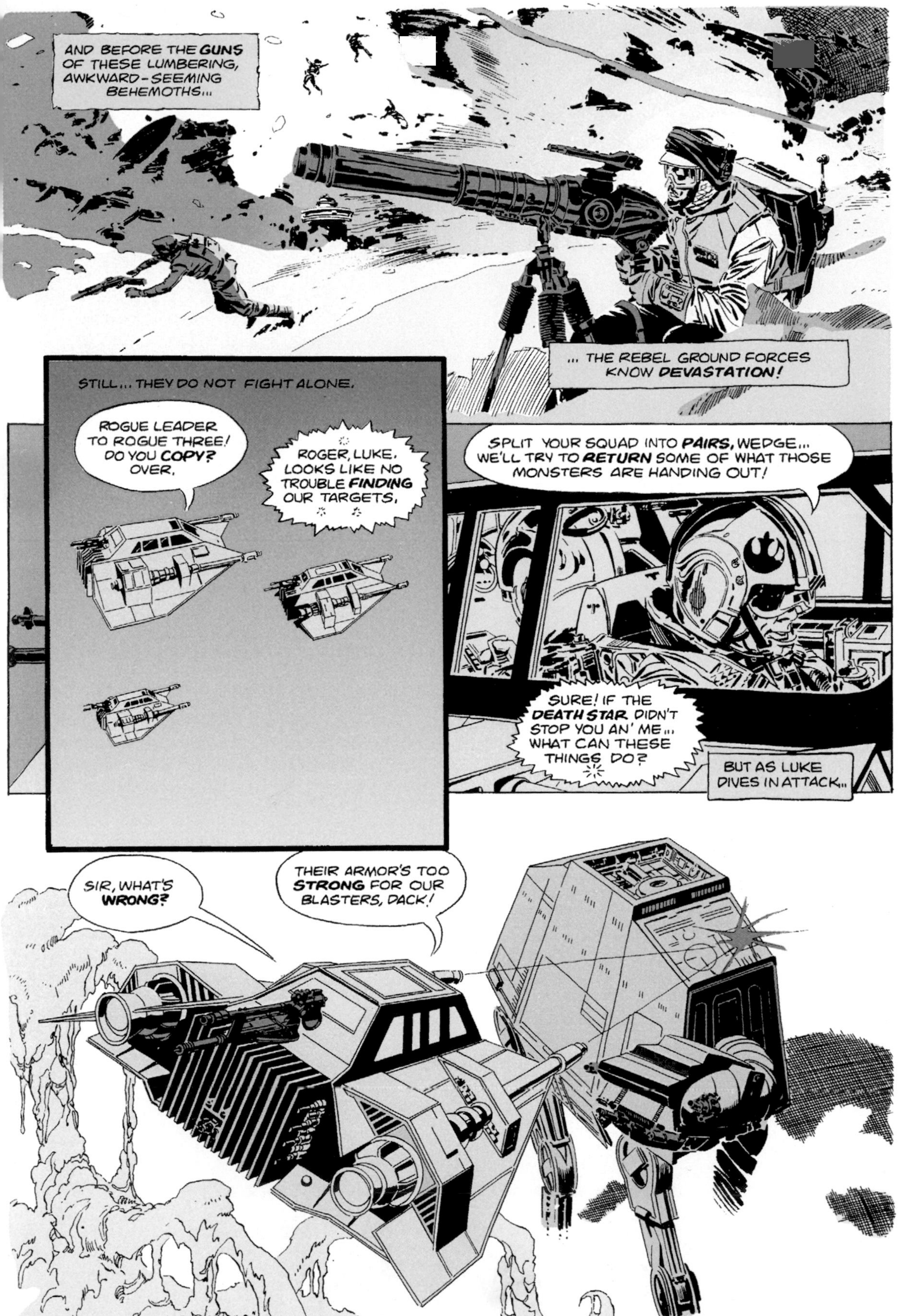
AND BEFORE THE GUNS OF THESE LUMBERING, AWKWARD-SEEMING BEHEMOTHS...
... THE REBEL GROUND FORCES KNOW DEVASTATION!
STILL... THEY DO NOT FIGHT ALONE.
ROGUE LEADER TO ROGUE THREE! DO YOU COPY? OVER.
ROGER, LUKE. LOOKS LIKE NO TROUBLE FINDING OUR TARGETS.
SPLIT YOUR SQUAD INTO PAIRS, WEDGE... WE'LL TRY TO RETURN SOME OF WHAT THOSE MONSTERS ARE HANDING OUT!
SURE! IF THE DEATH STAR DIDN'T STOP YOU AN' ME... WHAT CAN THESE THINGS DO?
BUT AS LUKE DIVES IN ATTACK...
SIR, WHAT'S WRONG?
THEIR ARMOR'S TOO STRONG FOR OUR BLASTERS, DACK!

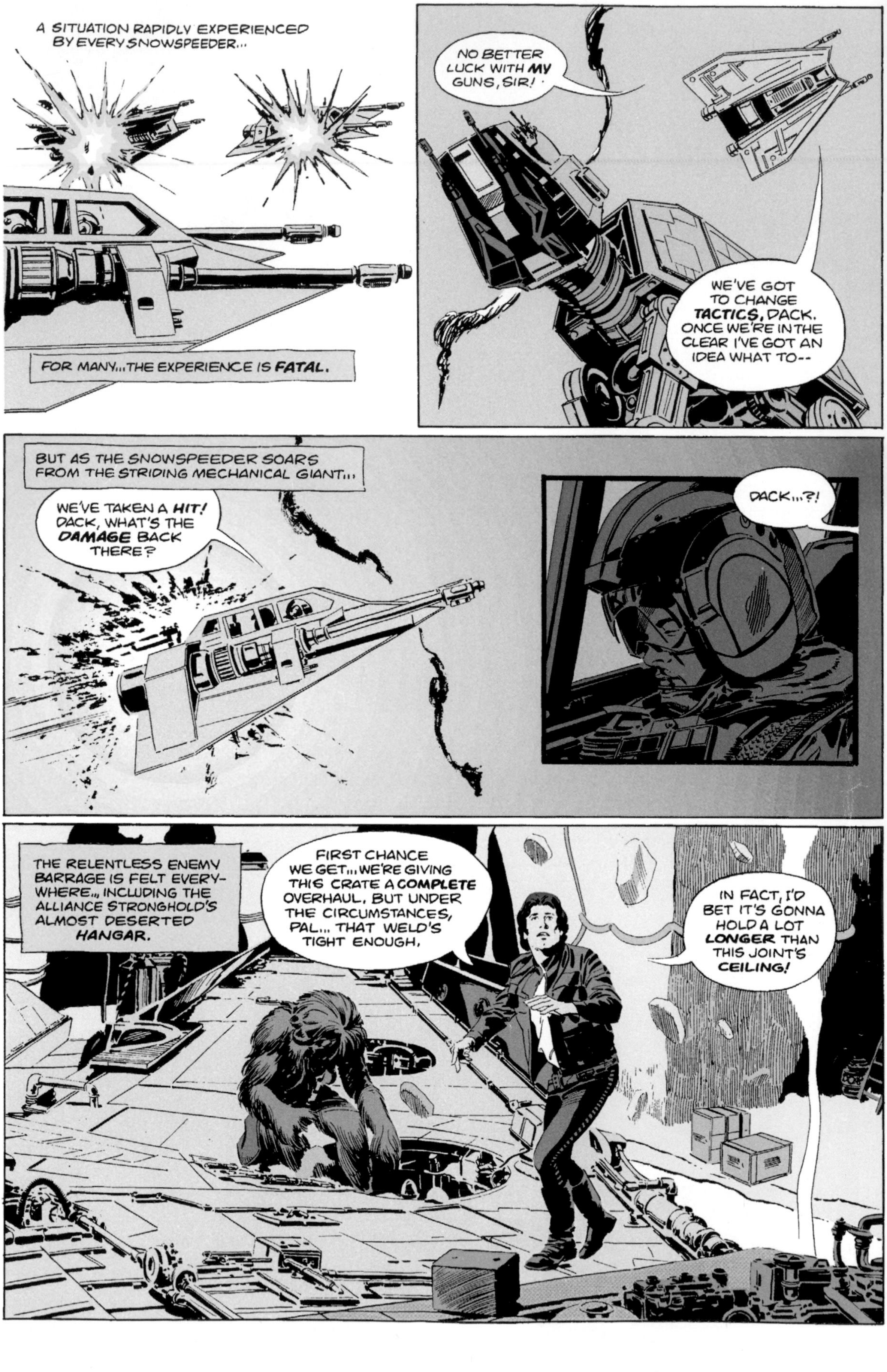
A SITUATION RAPIDLY EXPERIENCED BY EVERY SNOWSPEEDER...
FOR MANY... THE EXPERIENCE IS **FATAL.**
NO BETTER LUCK WITH **MY** GUNS, SIR!
WE'VE GOT TO CHANGE **TACTICS,** DACK. ONCE WE'RE IN THE CLEAR I'VE GOT AN IDEA WHAT TO--
BUT AS THE SNOWSPEEDER SOARS FROM THE STRIDING MECHANICAL GIANT...
WE'VE TAKEN A **HIT!** DACK, WHAT'S THE **DAMAGE** BACK THERE?
DACK...?!
THE RELENTLESS ENEMY BARRAGE IS FELT EVERYWHERE... INCLUDING THE ALLIANCE STRONGHOLD'S ALMOST DESERTED **HANGAR.**
FIRST CHANCE WE GET... WE'RE GIVING THIS CRATE A **COMPLETE** OVERHAUL. BUT UNDER THE CIRCUMSTANCES, PAL... THAT WELD'S TIGHT ENOUGH.
IN FACT, I'D BET IT'S GONNA HOLD A LOT **LONGER** THAN THIS JOINT'S **CEILING!**

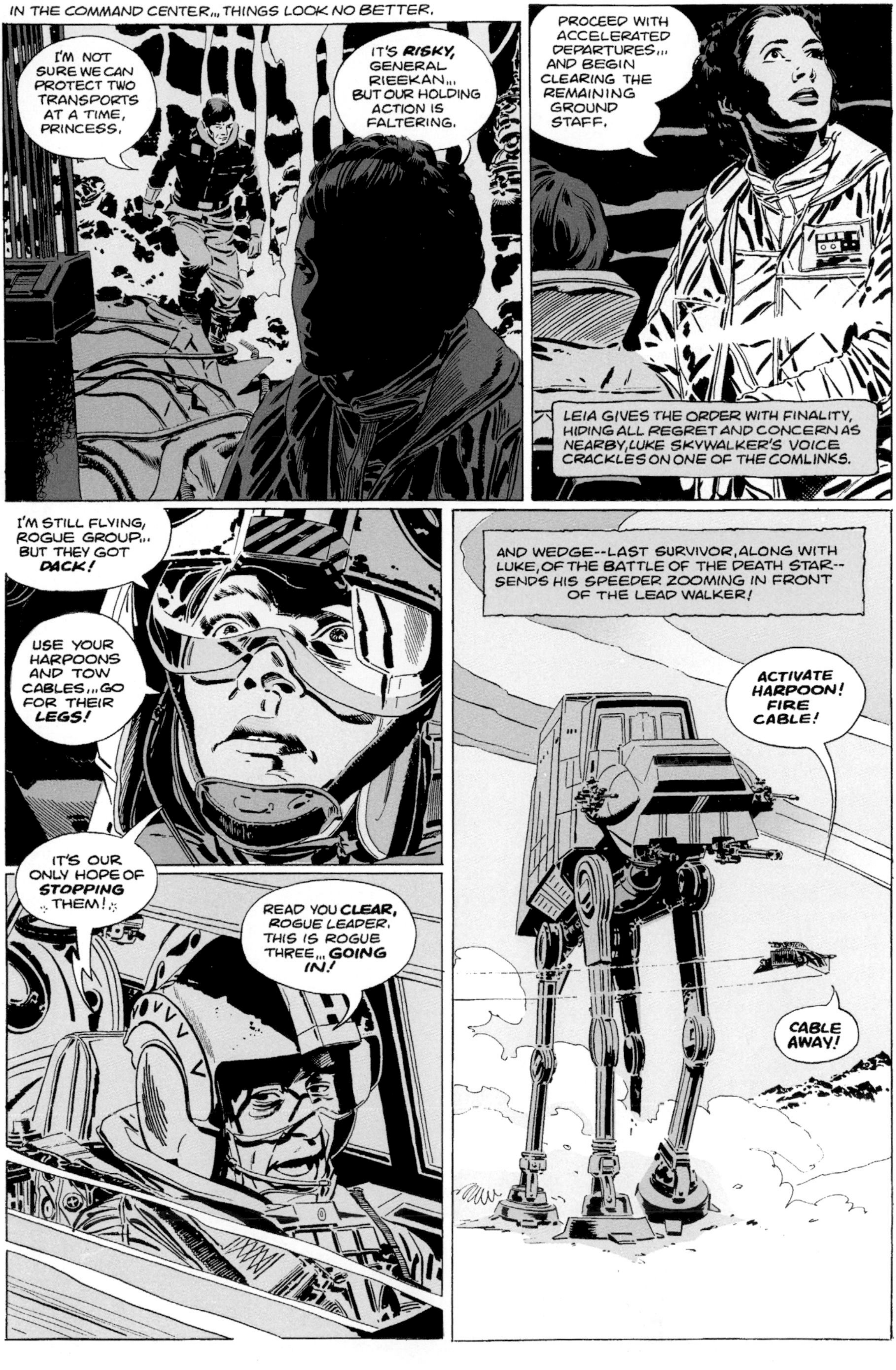
IN THE COMMAND CENTER... THINGS LOOK NO BETTER.
I'M NOT SURE WE CAN PROTECT TWO TRANSPORTS AT A TIME, PRINCESS.
IT'S RISKY, GENERAL RIEEKAN... BUT OUR HOLDING ACTION IS FALTERING.
PROCEED WITH ACCELERATED DEPARTURES... AND BEGIN CLEARING THE REMAINING GROUND STAFF.
LEIA GIVES THE ORDER WITH FINALITY, HIDING ALL REGRET AND CONCERN AS NEARBY, LUKE SKYWALKER'S VOICE CRACKLES ON ONE OF THE COMLINKS.
I'M STILL FLYING, ROGUE GROUP... BUT THEY GOT DACK!
USE YOUR HARPOONS AND TOW CABLES... GO FOR THEIR LEGS!
IT'S OUR ONLY HOPE OF STOPPING THEM!
READ YOU CLEAR, ROGUE LEADER. THIS IS ROGUE THREE... GOING IN!
AND WEDGE--LAST SURVIVOR, ALONG WITH LUKE, OF THE BATTLE OF THE DEATH STAR--SENDS HIS SPEEDER ZOOMING IN FRONT OF THE LEAD WALKER!
ACTIVATE HARPOON! FIRE CABLE!
CABLE AWAY!

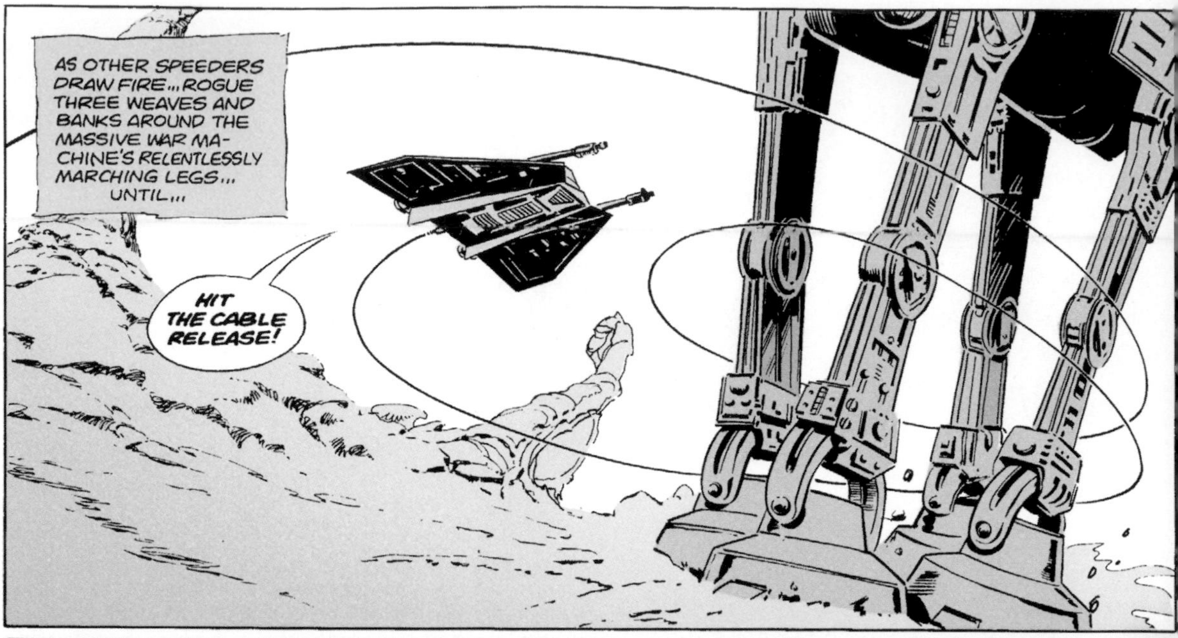
AS OTHER SPEEDERS DRAW FIRE... ROGUE THREE WEAVES AND BANKS AROUND THE MASSIVE WAR MACHINE'S RELENTLESSLY MARCHING LEGS... UNTIL...
HIT THE CABLE RELEASE!

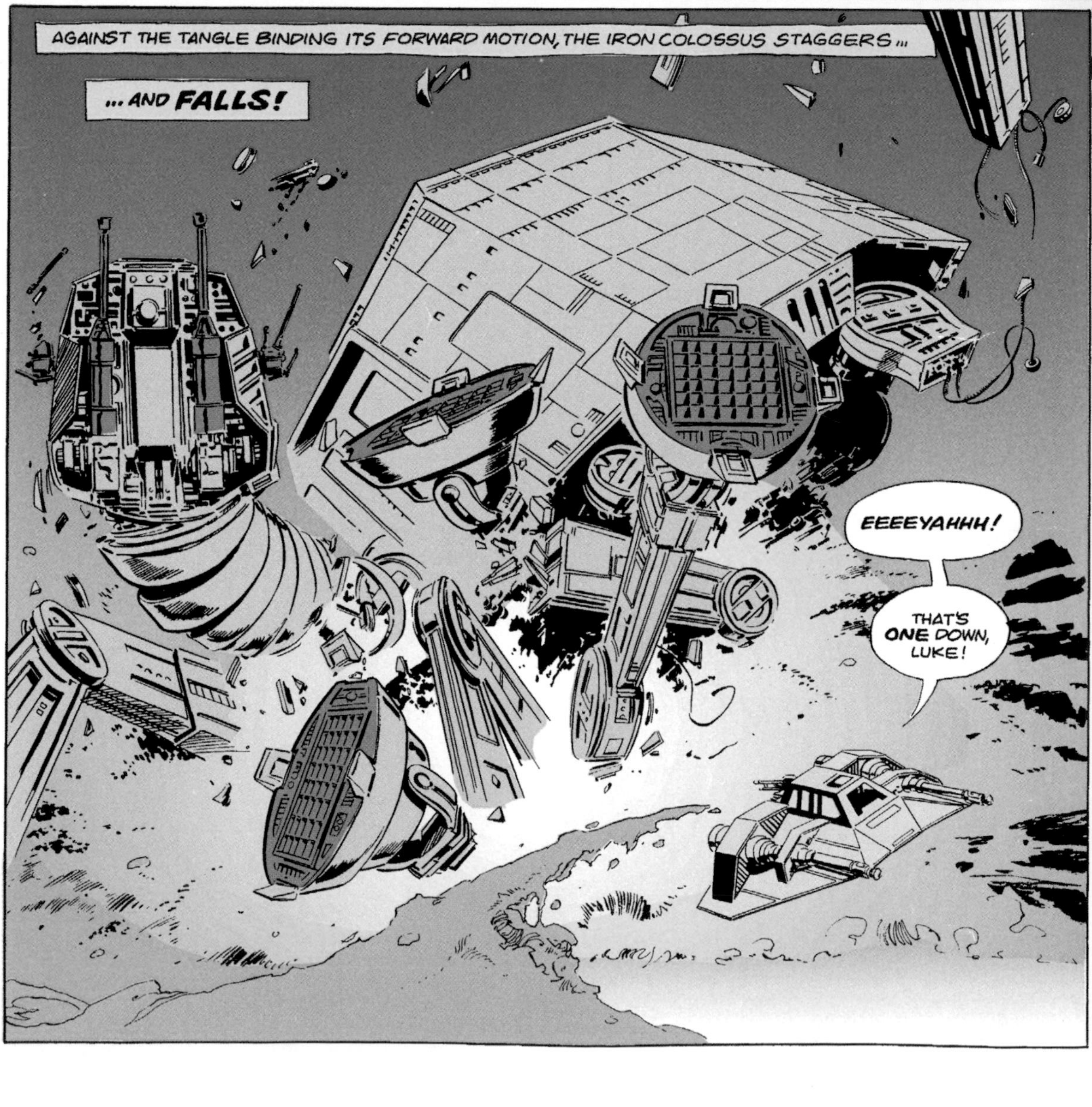
AGAINST THE TANGLE BINDING ITS FORWARD MOTION, THE IRON COLOSSUS STAGGERS...
...AND FALLS!
EEEEYAHHH!
THAT'S ONE DOWN, LUKE!

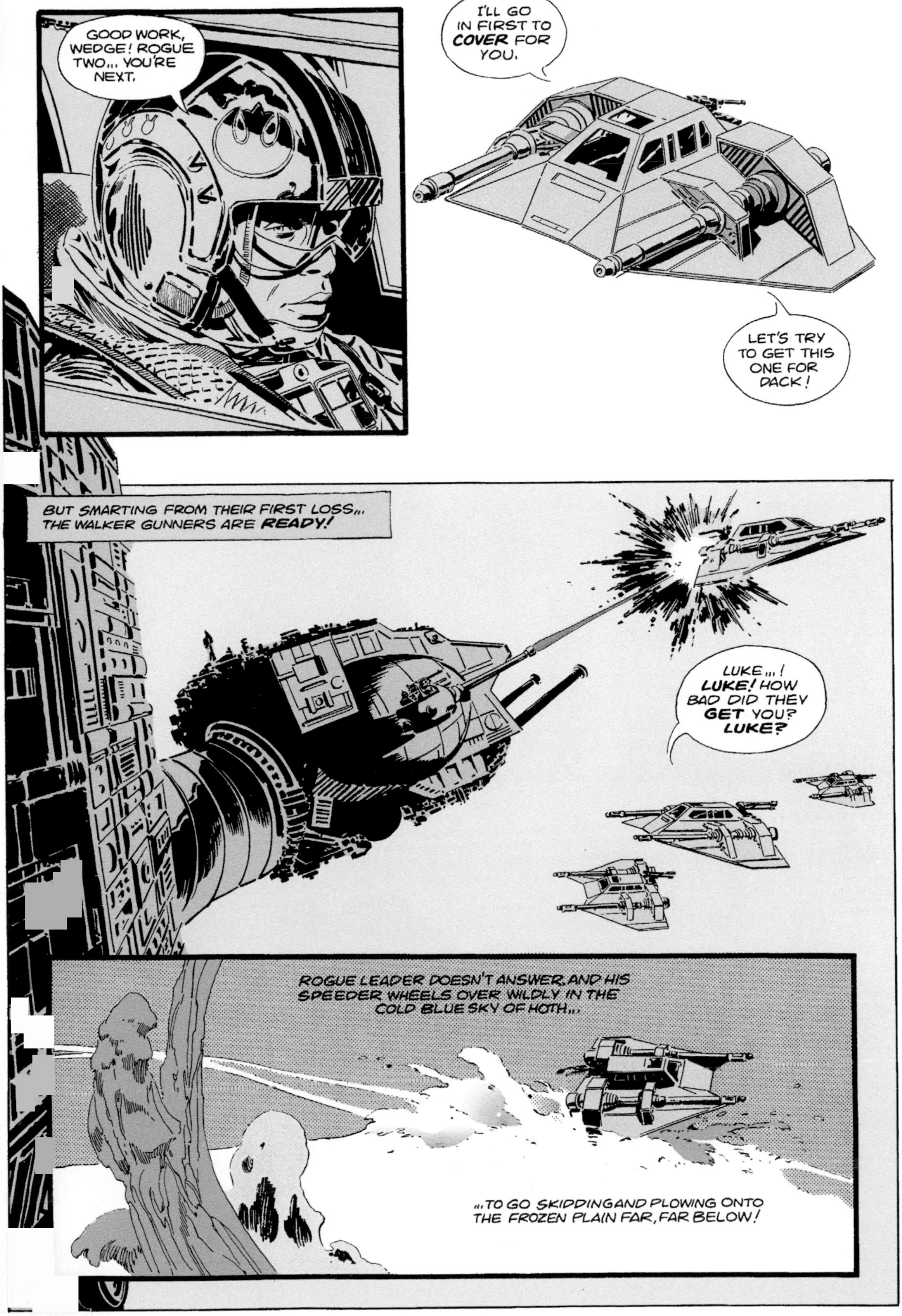
GOOD WORK, WEDGE! ROGUE TWO... YOU'RE NEXT.
I'LL GO IN FIRST TO COVER FOR YOU.
LET'S TRY TO GET THIS ONE FOR DACK!
BUT SMARTING FROM THEIR FIRST LOSS... THE WALKER GUNNERS ARE READY!
LUKE...! LUKE! HOW BAD DID THEY GET YOU? LUKE?
ROGUE LEADER DOESN'T ANSWER, AND HIS SPEEDER WHEELS OVER WILDLY IN THE COLD BLUE SKY OF HOTH...
...TO GO SKIDDING AND PLOWING ONTO THE FROZEN PLAIN FAR, FAR BELOW!

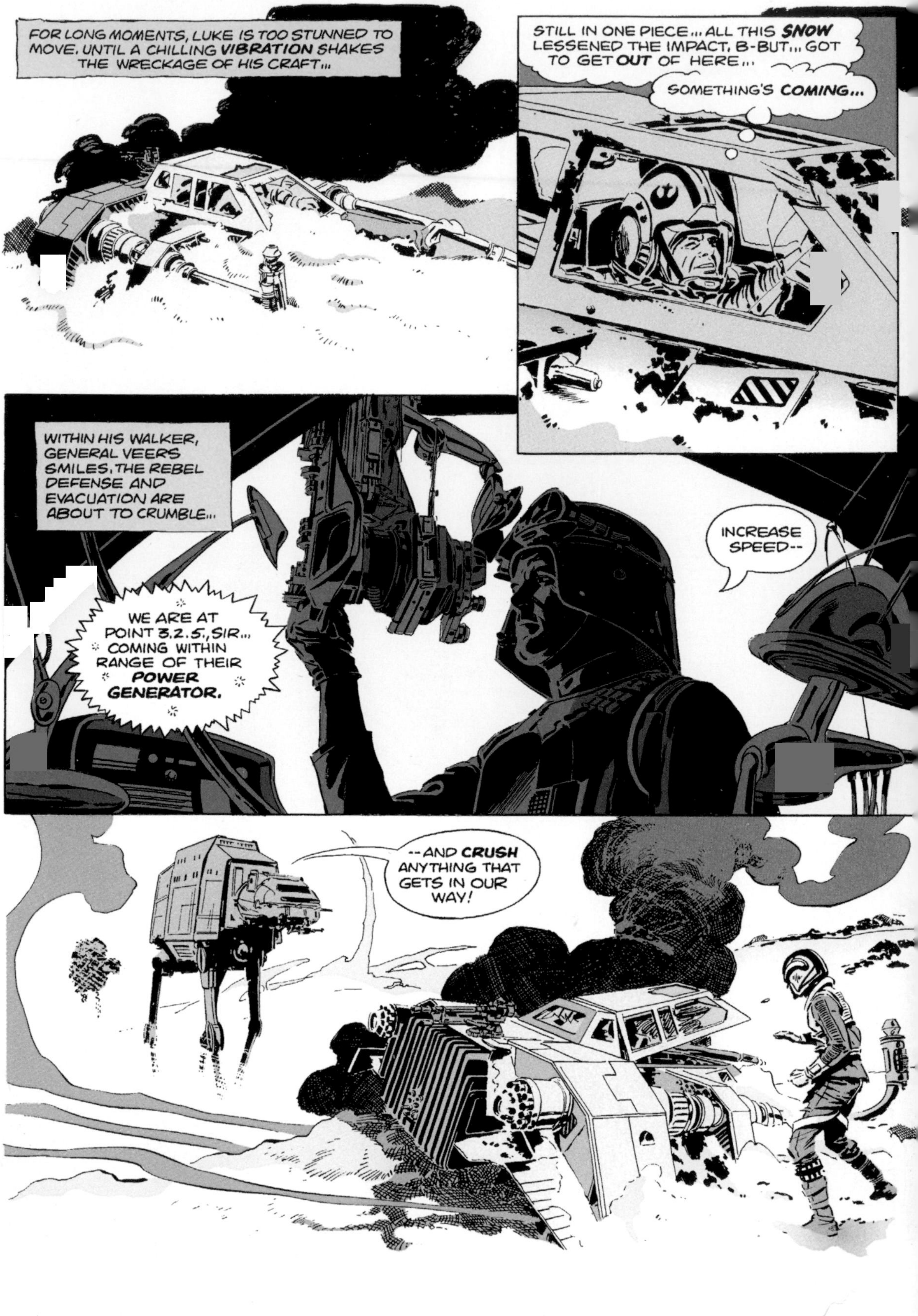
FOR LONG MOMENTS, LUKE IS TOO STUNNED TO MOVE. UNTIL A CHILLING VIBRATION SHAKES THE WRECKAGE OF HIS CRAFT...
STILL IN ONE PIECE... ALL THIS SNOW LESSENED THE IMPACT. B-BUT... GOT TO GET OUT OF HERE...
SOMETHING'S COMING...
WITHIN HIS WALKER, GENERAL VEERS SMILES. THE REBEL DEFENSE AND EVACUATION ARE ABOUT TO CRUMBLE...
WE ARE AT POINT 3.2.5., SIR... COMING WITHIN RANGE OF THEIR POWER GENERATOR.
INCREASE SPEED--
--AND CRUSH ANYTHING THAT GETS IN OUR WAY!

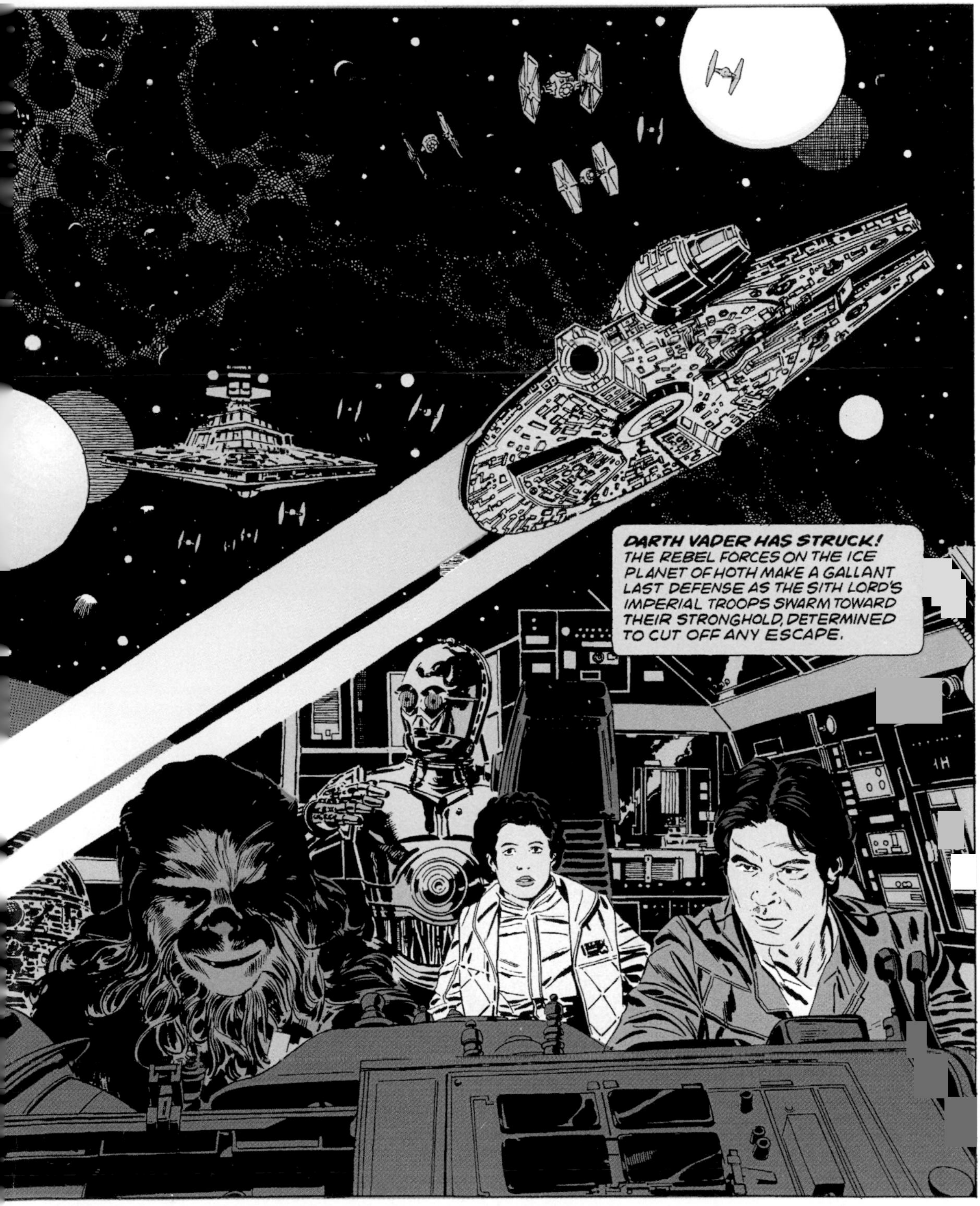
DARTH VADER HAS STRUCK! THE REBEL FORCES ON THE ICE PLANET OF HOTH MAKE A GALLANT LAST DEFENSE AS THE SITH LORD'S IMPERIAL TROOPS SWARM TOWARD THEIR STRONGHOLD, DETERMINED TO CUT OFF ANY ESCAPE.

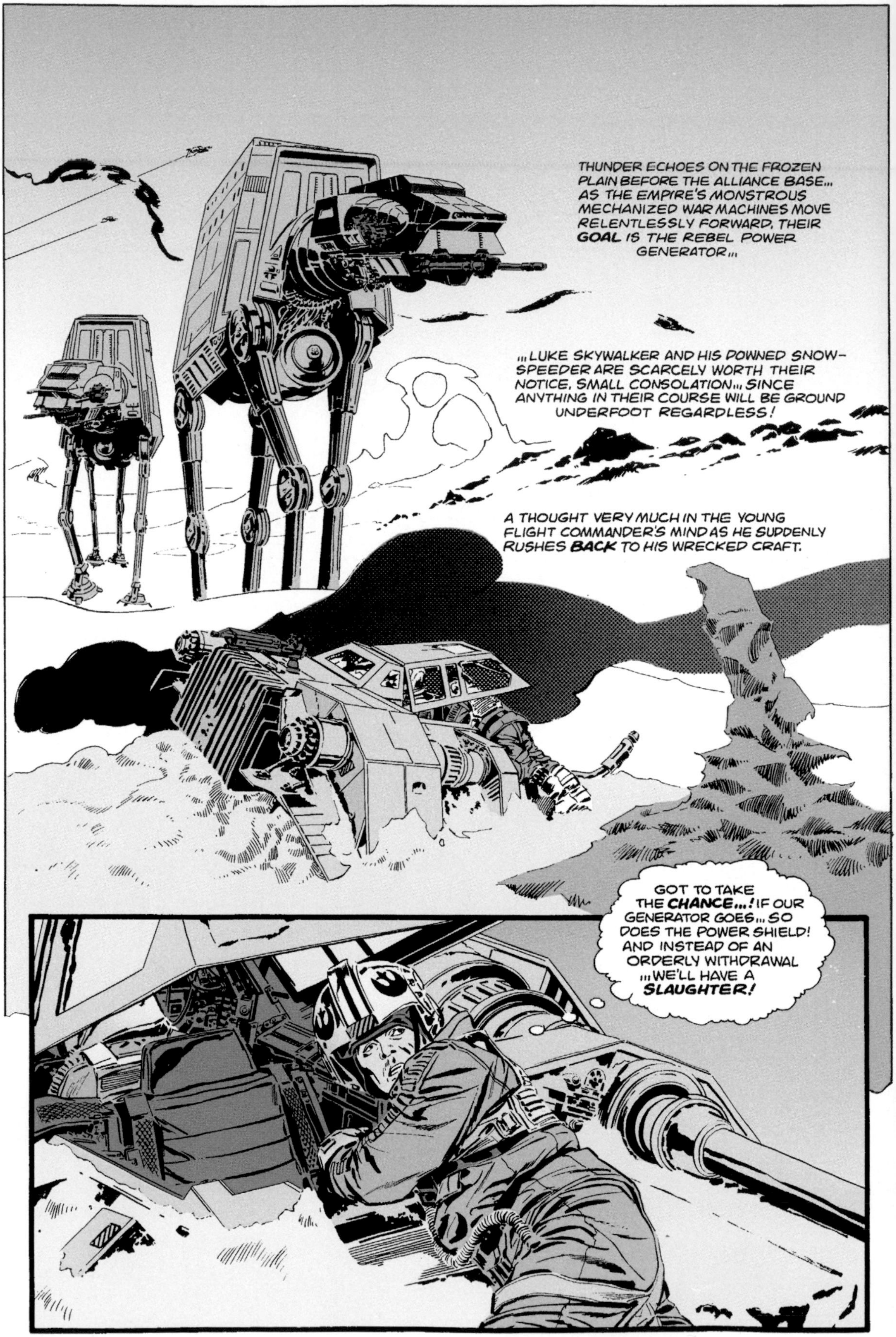
THUNDER ECHOES ON THE FROZEN PLAIN BEFORE THE ALLIANCE BASE... AS THE EMPIRE'S MONSTROUS MECHANIZED WAR MACHINES MOVE RELENTLESSLY FORWARD. THEIR GOAL IS THE REBEL POWER GENERATOR...
...LUKE SKYWALKER AND HIS DOWNED SNOW-SPEEDER ARE SCARCELY WORTH THEIR NOTICE. SMALL CONSOLATION... SINCE ANYTHING IN THEIR COURSE WILL BE GROUND UNDERFOOT REGARDLESS!
A THOUGHT VERY MUCH IN THE YOUNG FLIGHT COMMANDER'S MIND AS HE SUDDENLY RUSHES BACK TO HIS WRECKED CRAFT.
GOT TO TAKE THE CHANCE...! IF OUR GENERATOR GOES... SO DOES THE POWER SHIELD! AND INSTEAD OF AN ORDERLY WITHDRAWAL ...WE'LL HAVE A SLAUGHTER!

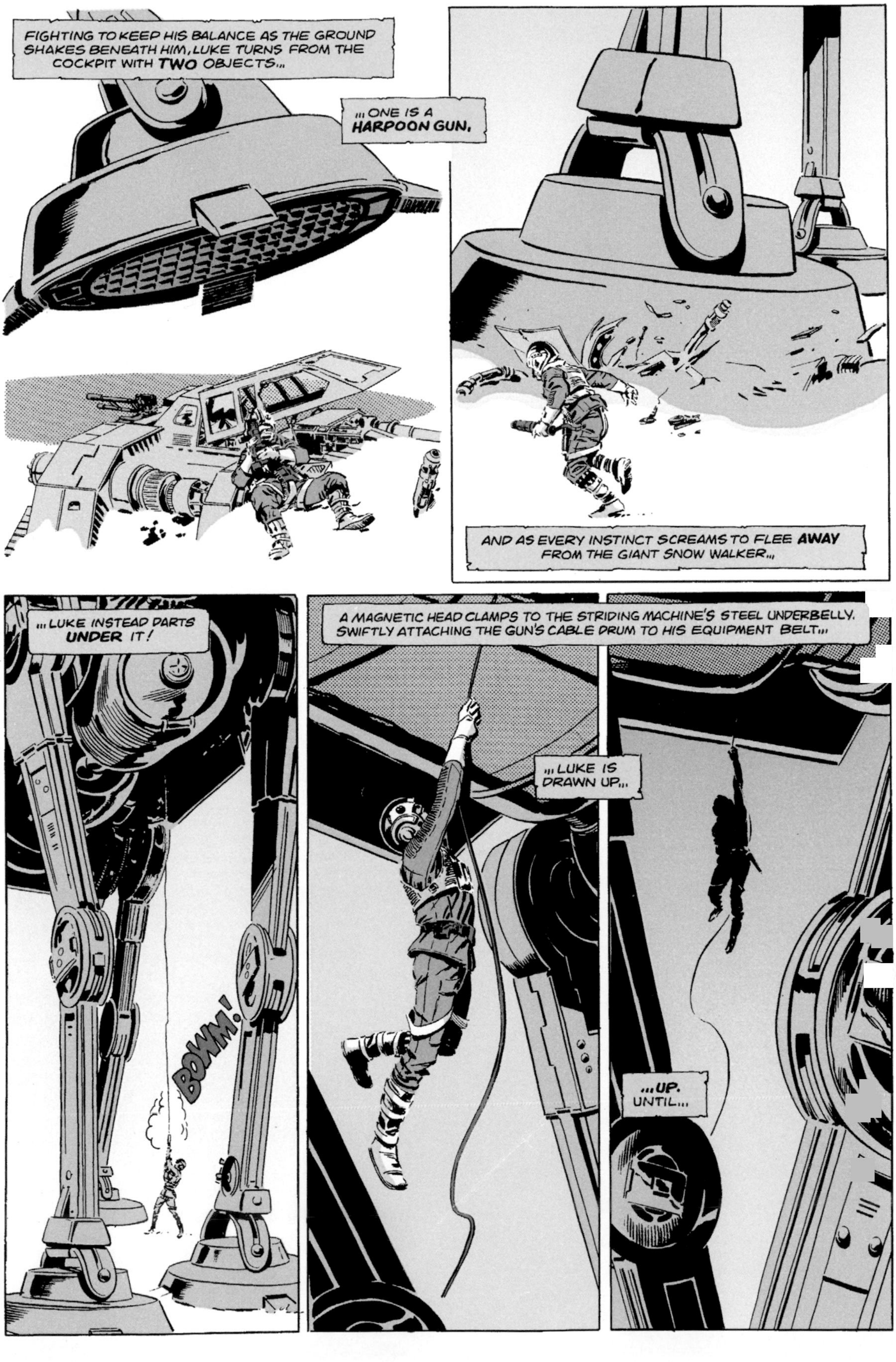
FIGHTING TO KEEP HIS BALANCE AS THE GROUND SHAKES BENEATH HIM, LUKE TURNS FROM THE COCKPIT WITH TWO OBJECTS...
...ONE IS A HARPOON GUN.
AND AS EVERY INSTINCT SCREAMS TO FLEE AWAY FROM THE GIANT SNOW WALKER...
...LUKE INSTEAD DARTS UNDER IT!
BOWM!
A MAGNETIC HEAD CLAMPS TO THE STRIDING MACHINE'S STEEL UNDERBELLY. SWIFTLY ATTACHING THE GUN'S CABLE DRUM TO HIS EQUIPMENT BELT...
...LUKE IS DRAWN UP...
...UP. UNTIL...

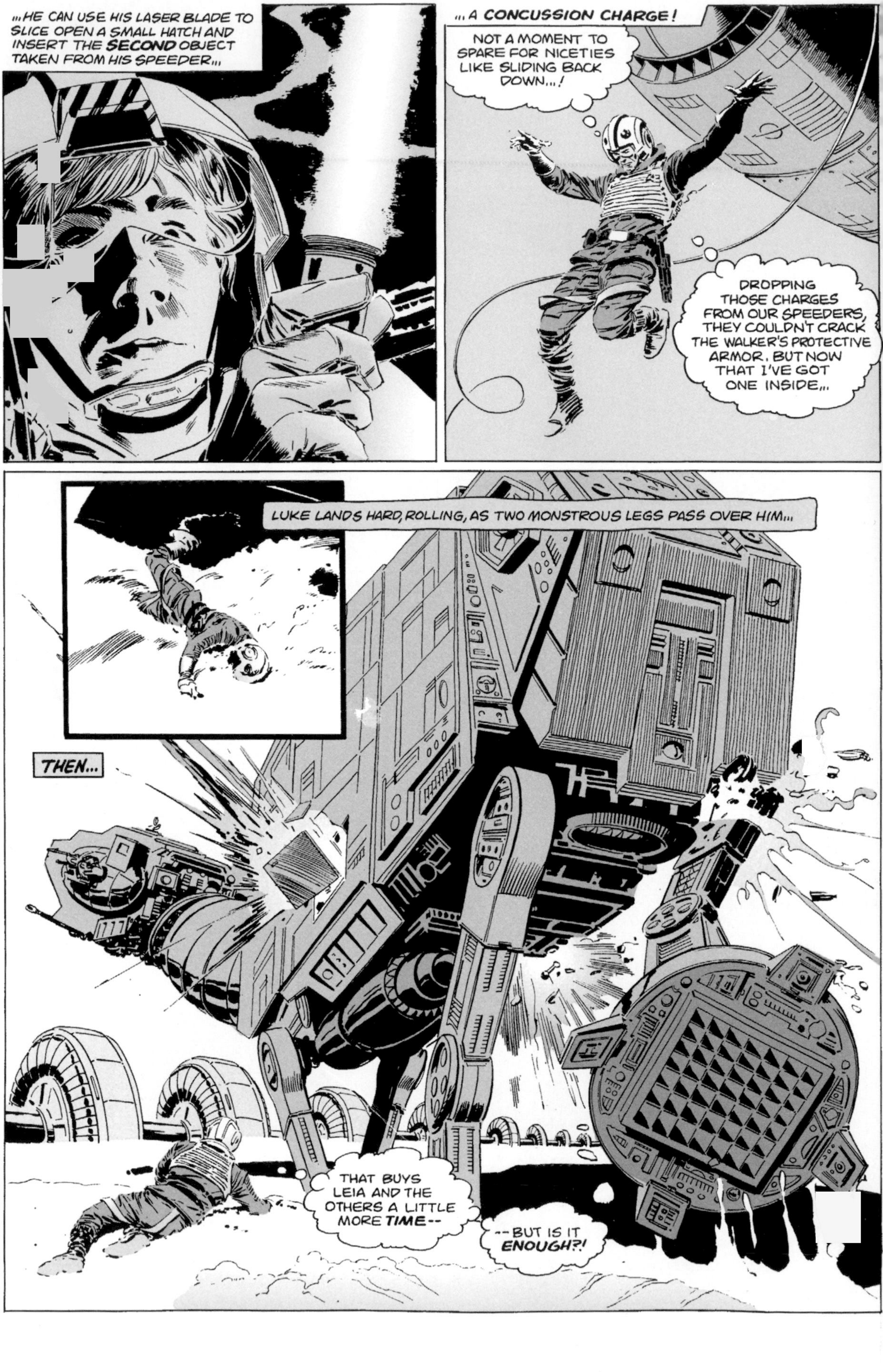
...HE CAN USE HIS LASER BLADE TO SLICE OPEN A SMALL HATCH AND INSERT THE **SECOND** OBJECT TAKEN FROM HIS SPEEDER...
...A **CONCUSSION CHARGE!**
NOT A MOMENT TO SPARE FOR NICETIES LIKE SLIDING BACK DOWN...!
DROPPING THOSE CHARGES FROM OUR SPEEDERS, THEY COULDN'T CRACK THE WALKER'S PROTECTIVE ARMOR. BUT NOW THAT I'VE GOT ONE INSIDE...
LUKE LANDS HARD, ROLLING, AS TWO MONSTROUS LEGS PASS OVER HIM...
THEN...
THAT BUYS LEIA AND THE OTHERS A LITTLE MORE **TIME**--
--BUT IS IT **ENOUGH?!**

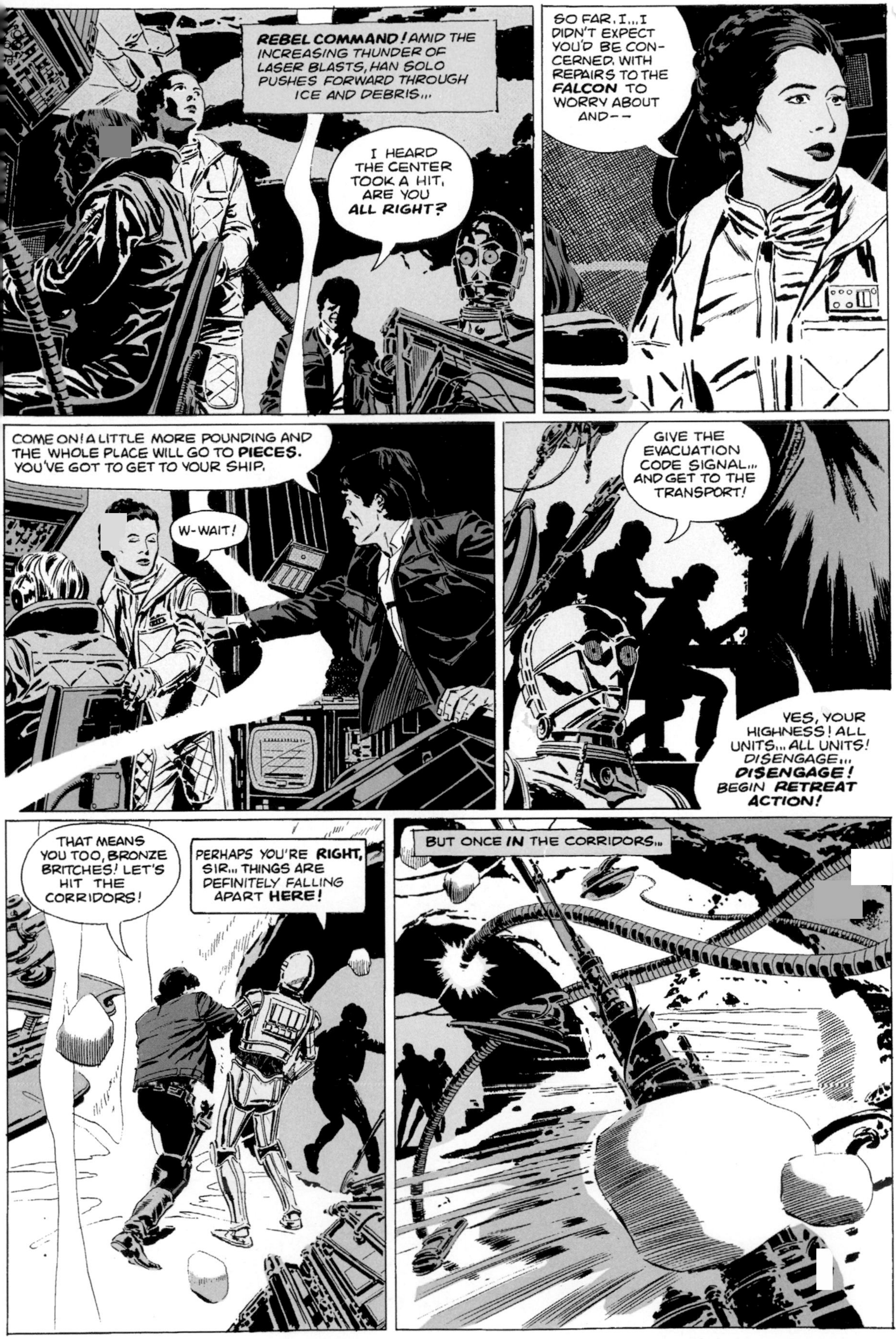
REBEL COMMAND! AMID THE INCREASING THUNDER OF LASER BLASTS, HAN SOLO PUSHES FORWARD THROUGH ICE AND DEBRIS...
I HEARD THE CENTER TOOK A HIT, ARE YOU ALL RIGHT?
SO FAR. I...I DIDN'T EXPECT YOU'D BE CONCERNED, WITH REPAIRS TO THE FALCON TO WORRY ABOUT AND--
COME ON! A LITTLE MORE POUNDING AND THE WHOLE PLACE WILL GO TO PIECES. YOU'VE GOT TO GET TO YOUR SHIP.
W-WAIT!
GIVE THE EVACUATION CODE SIGNAL... AND GET TO THE TRANSPORT!
YES, YOUR HIGHNESS! ALL UNITS... ALL UNITS! DISENGAGE... DISENGAGE! BEGIN RETREAT ACTION!
THAT MEANS YOU TOO, BRONZE BRITCHES! LET'S HIT THE CORRIDORS!
PERHAPS YOU'RE RIGHT, SIR... THINGS ARE DEFINITELY FALLING APART HERE!
BUT ONCE IN THE CORRIDORS...

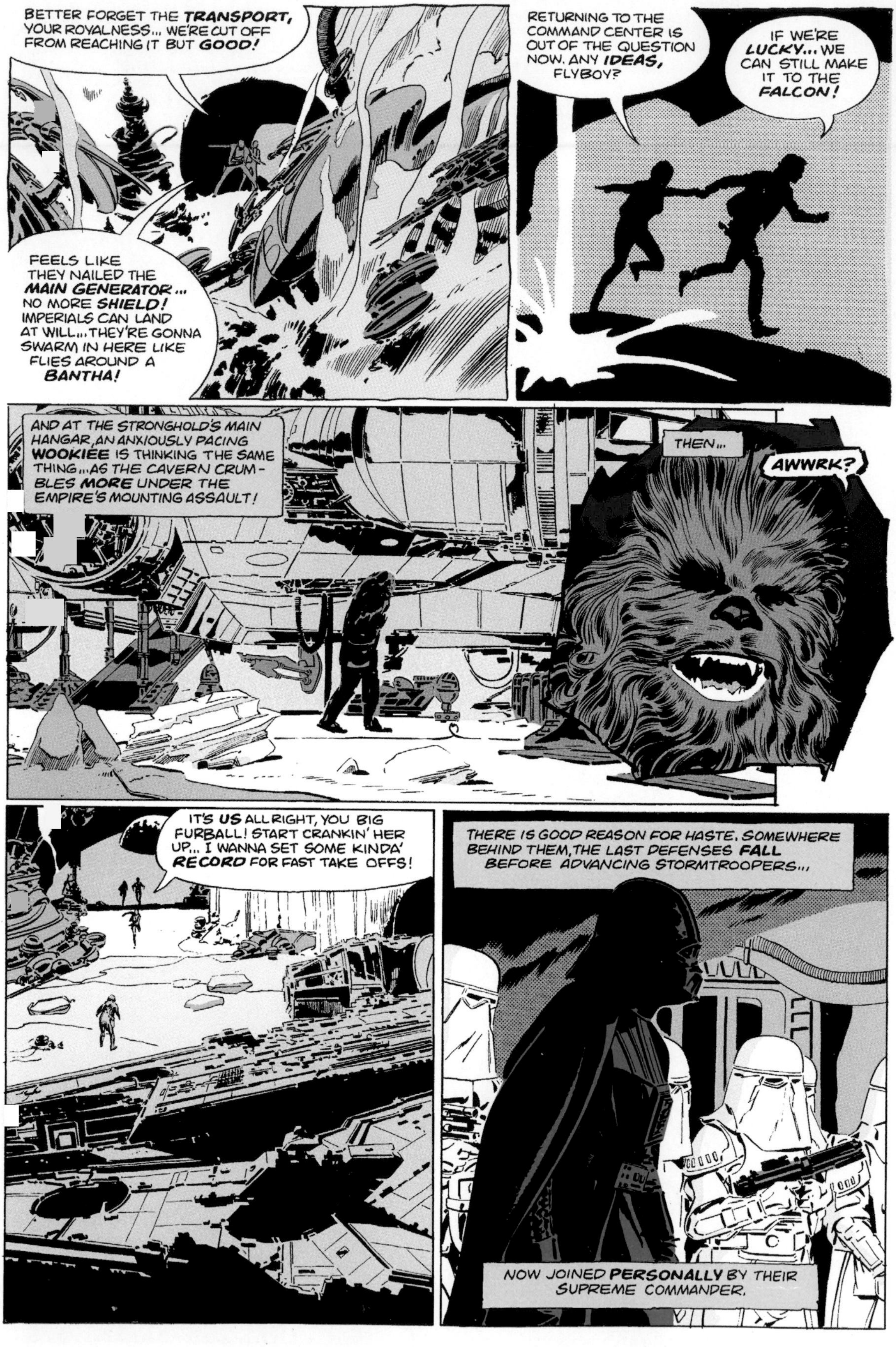
BETTER FORGET THE TRANSPORT, YOUR ROYALNESS... WE'RE CUT OFF FROM REACHING IT BUT GOOD!
FEELS LIKE THEY NAILED THE MAIN GENERATOR... NO MORE SHIELD! IMPERIALS CAN LAND AT WILL... THEY'RE GONNA SWARM IN HERE LIKE FLIES AROUND A BANTHA!
RETURNING TO THE COMMAND CENTER IS OUT OF THE QUESTION NOW. ANY IDEAS, FLYBOY?
IF WE'RE LUCKY... WE CAN STILL MAKE IT TO THE FALCON!
AND AT THE STRONGHOLD'S MAIN HANGAR, AN ANXIOUSLY PACING WOOKIEE IS THINKING THE SAME THING... AS THE CAVERN CRUMBLES MORE UNDER THE EMPIRE'S MOUNTING ASSAULT!
THEN...
AWWRK?
IT'S US ALL RIGHT, YOU BIG FURBALL! START CRANKIN' HER UP... I WANNA SET SOME KINDA' RECORD FOR FAST TAKE OFFS!
THERE IS GOOD REASON FOR HASTE. SOMEWHERE BEHIND THEM, THE LAST DEFENSES FALL BEFORE ADVANCING STORMTROOPERS...
NOW JOINED PERSONALLY BY THEIR SUPREME COMMANDER.

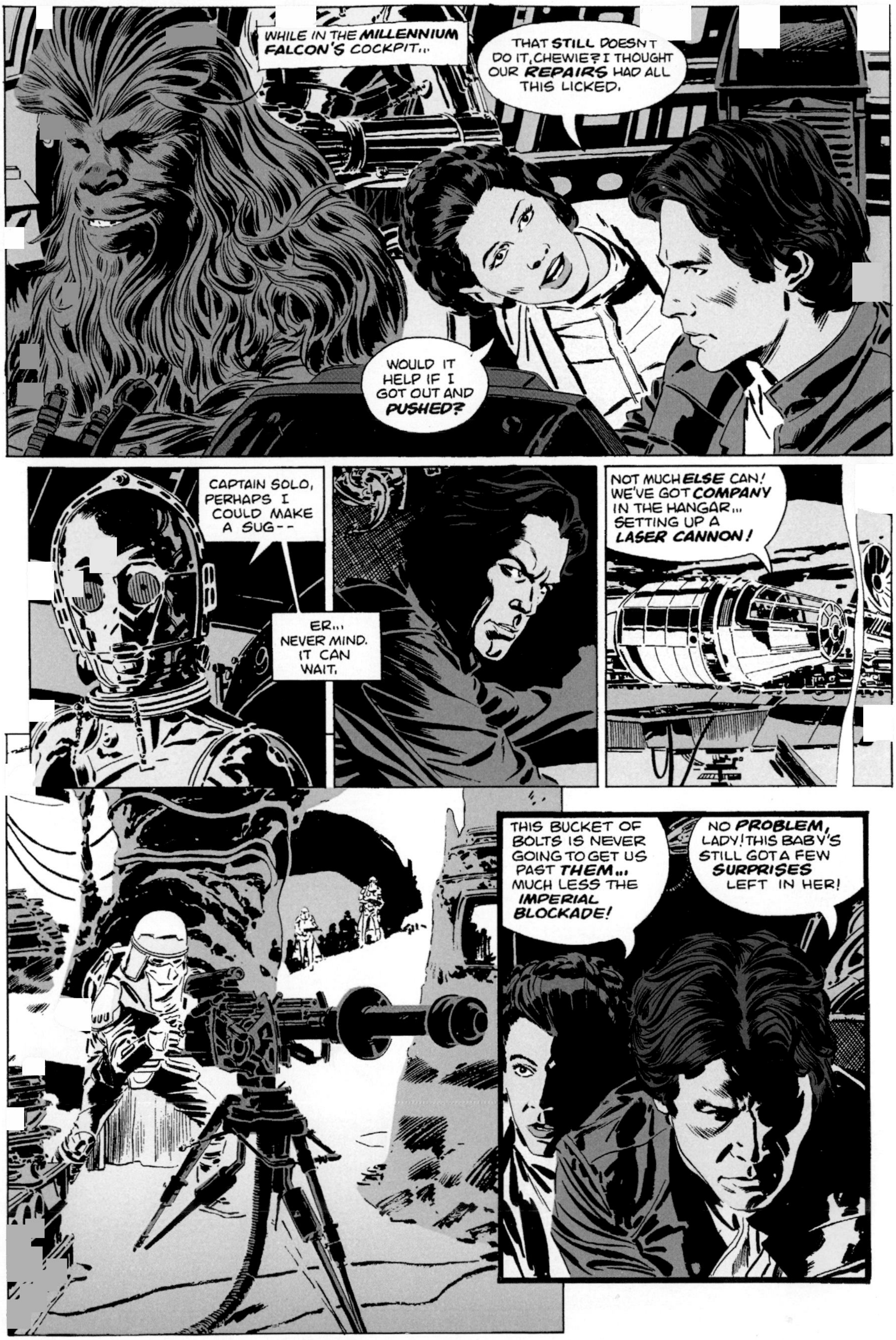
WHILE IN THE MILLENNIUM FALCON'S COCKPIT...
THAT STILL DOESN'T DO IT, CHEWIE? I THOUGHT OUR REPAIRS HAD ALL THIS LICKED.
WOULD IT HELP IF I GOT OUT AND PUSHED?
CAPTAIN SOLO, PERHAPS I COULD MAKE A SUG--
ER... NEVER MIND. IT CAN WAIT.
NOT MUCH ELSE CAN! WE'VE GOT COMPANY IN THE HANGAR... SETTING UP A LASER CANNON!
THIS BUCKET OF BOLTS IS NEVER GOING TO GET US PAST THEM... MUCH LESS THE IMPERIAL BLOCKADE!
NO PROBLEM, LADY! THIS BABY'S STILL GOT A FEW SURPRISES LEFT IN HER!

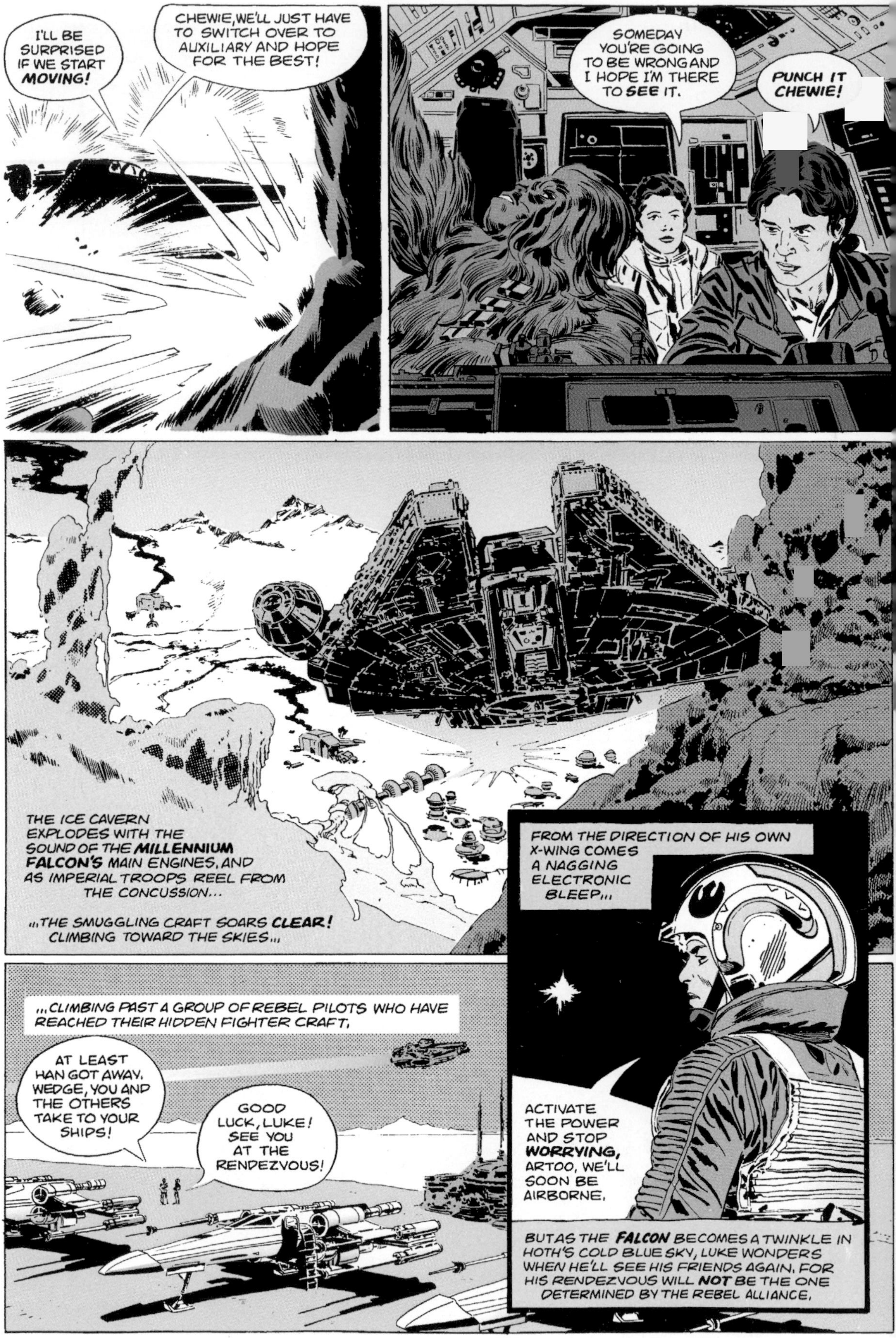
I'LL BE SURPRISED IF WE START MOVING!
CHEWIE, WE'LL JUST HAVE TO SWITCH OVER TO AUXILIARY AND HOPE FOR THE BEST!
SOMEDAY YOU'RE GOING TO BE WRONG AND I HOPE I'M THERE TO SEE IT.
PUNCH IT CHEWIE!
THE ICE CAVERN EXPLODES WITH THE SOUND OF THE MILLENNIUM FALCON'S MAIN ENGINES, AND AS IMPERIAL TROOPS REEL FROM THE CONCUSSION...
...THE SMUGGLING CRAFT SOARS CLEAR! CLIMBING TOWARD THE SKIES...
...CLIMBING PAST A GROUP OF REBEL PILOTS WHO HAVE REACHED THEIR HIDDEN FIGHTER CRAFT.
AT LEAST HAN GOT AWAY. WEDGE, YOU AND THE OTHERS TAKE TO YOUR SHIPS!
GOOD LUCK, LUKE! SEE YOU AT THE RENDEZVOUS!
FROM THE DIRECTION OF HIS OWN X-WING COMES A NAGGING ELECTRONIC BLEEP...
ACTIVATE THE POWER AND STOP WORRYING, ARTOO, WE'LL SOON BE AIRBORNE.
BUT AS THE FALCON BECOMES A TWINKLE IN HOTH'S COLD BLUE SKY, LUKE WONDERS WHEN HE'LL SEE HIS FRIENDS AGAIN. FOR HIS RENDEZVOUS WILL NOT BE THE ONE DETERMINED BY THE REBEL ALLIANCE.

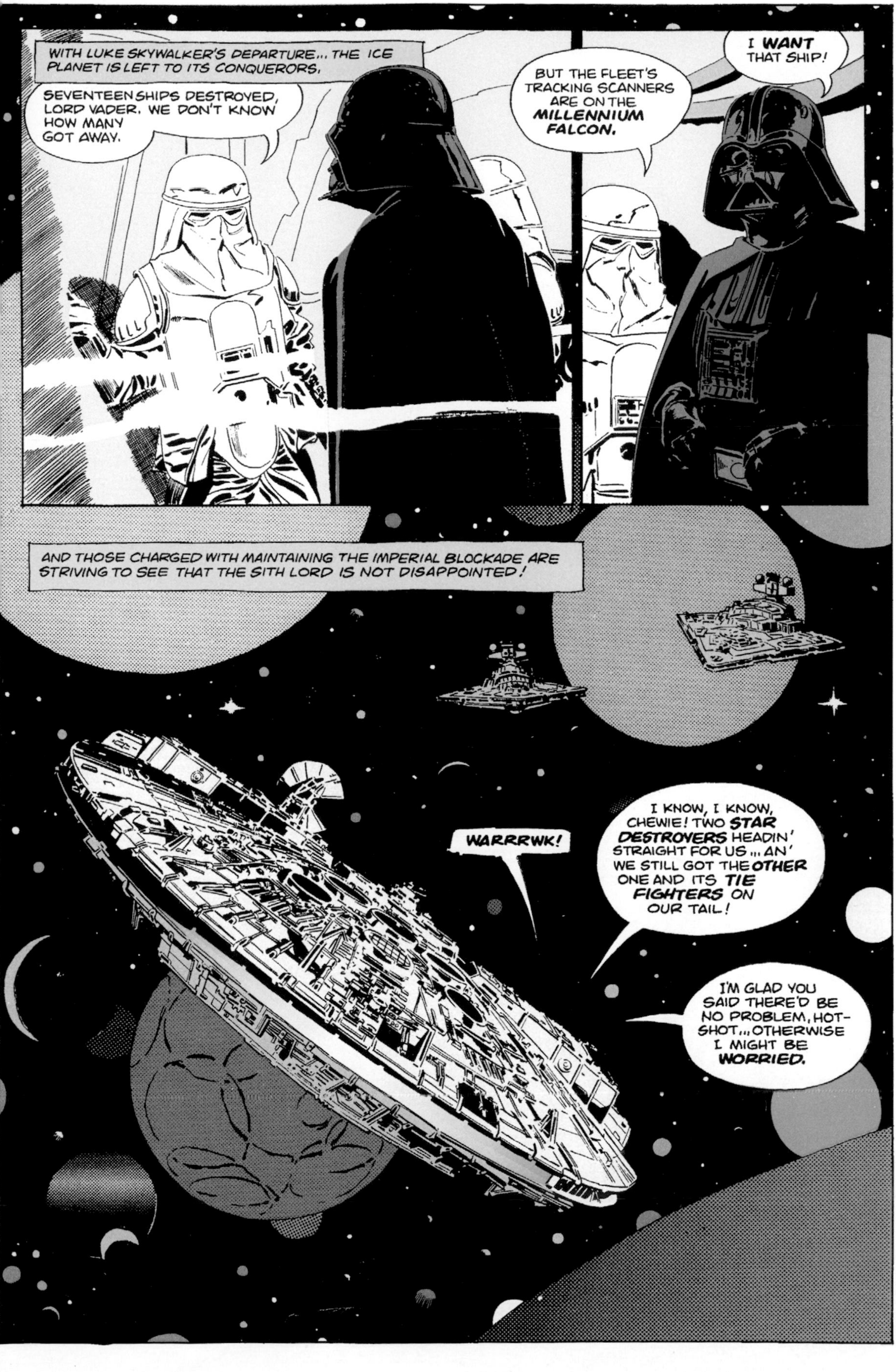
WITH LUKE SKYWALKER'S DEPARTURE... THE ICE PLANET IS LEFT TO ITS CONQUERORS.
SEVENTEEN SHIPS DESTROYED, LORD VADER. WE DON'T KNOW HOW MANY GOT AWAY.
BUT THE FLEET'S TRACKING SCANNERS ARE ON THE MILLENNIUM FALCON.
I WANT THAT SHIP!
AND THOSE CHARGED WITH MAINTAINING THE IMPERIAL BLOCKADE ARE STRIVING TO SEE THAT THE SITH LORD IS NOT DISAPPOINTED!
WARRRWK!
I KNOW, I KNOW, CHEWIE! TWO STAR DESTROYERS HEADIN' STRAIGHT FOR US... AN' WE STILL GOT THE OTHER ONE AND ITS TIE FIGHTERS ON OUR TAIL!
I'M GLAD YOU SAID THERE'D BE NO PROBLEM, HOT-SHOT... OTHERWISE I MIGHT BE WORRIED.

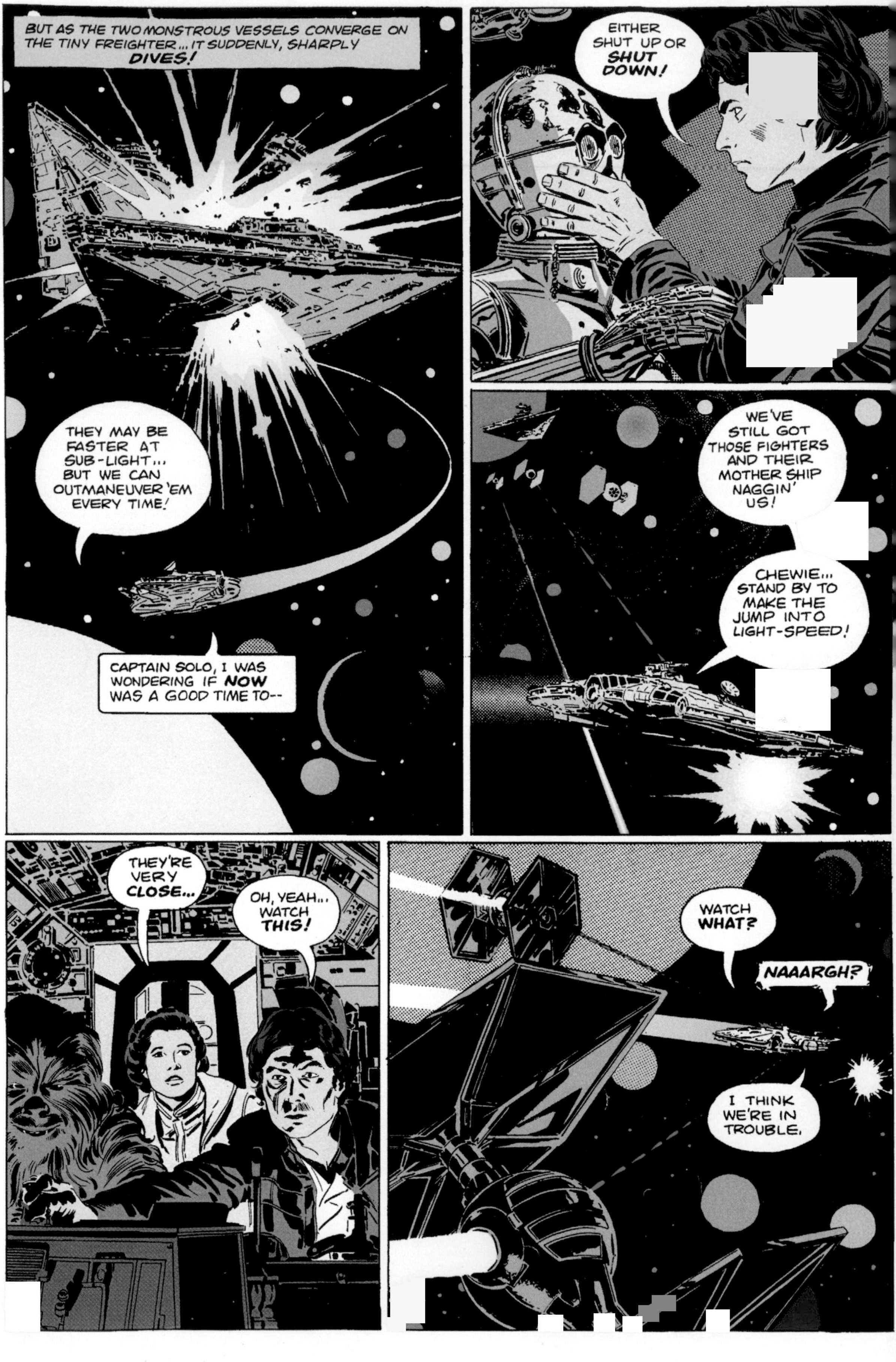
BUT AS THE TWO MONSTROUS VESSELS CONVERGE ON THE TINY FREIGHTER... IT SUDDENLY, SHARPLY DIVES!
EITHER SHUT UP OR SHUT DOWN!
THEY MAY BE FASTER AT SUB-LIGHT... BUT WE CAN OUTMANEUVER 'EM EVERY TIME!
CAPTAIN SOLO, I WAS WONDERING IF NOW WAS A GOOD TIME TO--
WE'VE STILL GOT THOSE FIGHTERS AND THEIR MOTHER SHIP NAGGIN' US!
CHEWIE... STAND BY TO MAKE THE JUMP INTO LIGHT-SPEED!
THEY'RE VERY CLOSE...
OH, YEAH... WATCH THIS!
WATCH WHAT?
NAAARGH?
I THINK WE'RE IN TROUBLE.

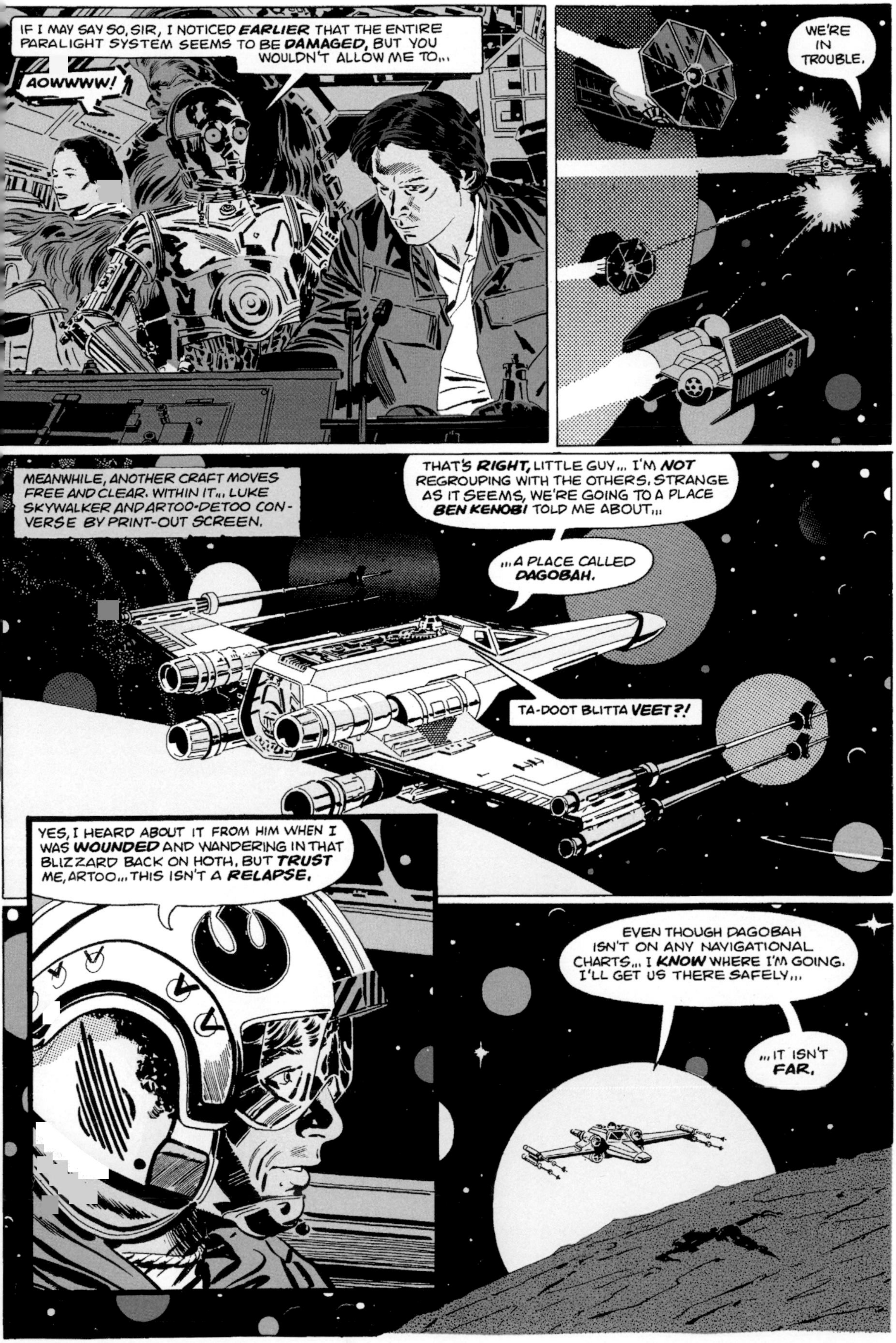

IF I MAY SAY SO, SIR, I NOTICED EARLIER THAT THE ENTIRE PARALIGHT SYSTEM SEEMS TO BE DAMAGED, BUT YOU WOULDN'T ALLOW ME TO...
AOWWWW!
WE'RE IN TROUBLE.
MEANWHILE, ANOTHER CRAFT MOVES FREE AND CLEAR. WITHIN IT... LUKE SKYWALKER AND ARTOO-DETOO CONVERSE BY PRINT-OUT SCREEN.
THAT'S RIGHT, LITTLE GUY... I'M NOT REGROUPING WITH THE OTHERS. STRANGE AS IT SEEMS, WE'RE GOING TO A PLACE BEN KENOBI TOLD ME ABOUT...
...A PLACE CALLED DAGOBAH.
TA-DOOT BLITTA VEET?!
YES, I HEARD ABOUT IT FROM HIM WHEN I WAS WOUNDED AND WANDERING IN THAT BLIZZARD BACK ON HOTH, BUT TRUST ME, ARTOO... THIS ISN'T A RELAPSE.
EVEN THOUGH DAGOBAH ISN'T ON ANY NAVIGATIONAL CHARTS... I KNOW WHERE I'M GOING. I'LL GET US THERE SAFELY...
...IT ISN'T FAR.

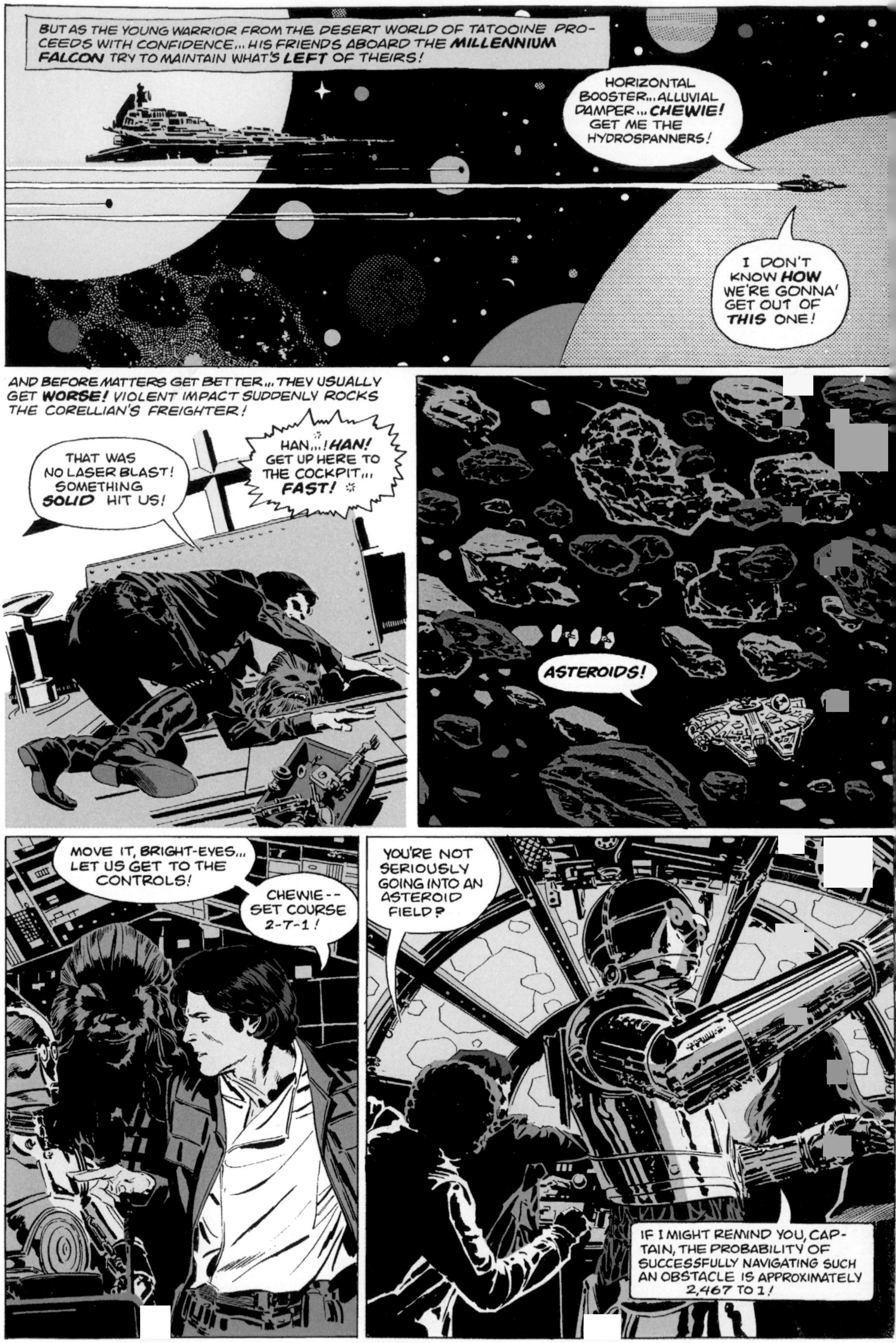
BUT AS THE YOUNG WARRIOR FROM THE DESERT WORLD OF TATOOINE PROCEEDS WITH CONFIDENCE... HIS FRIENDS ABOARD THE MILLENNIUM FALCON TRY TO MAINTAIN WHAT'S LEFT OF THEIRS!
HORIZONTAL BOOSTER... ALLUVIAL DAMPER... CHEWIE! GET ME THE HYDROSPANNERS!
I DON'T KNOW HOW WE'RE GONNA' GET OUT OF THIS ONE!
AND BEFORE MATTERS GET BETTER... THEY USUALLY GET WORSE! VIOLENT IMPACT SUDDENLY ROCKS THE CORELLIAN'S FREIGHTER!
THAT WAS NO LASER BLAST! SOMETHING SOLID HIT US!
HAN...! HAN! GET UP HERE TO THE COCKPIT... FAST!
ASTEROIDS!
MOVE IT, BRIGHT-EYES... LET US GET TO THE CONTROLS!
CHEWIE -- SET COURSE 2-7-1!
YOU'RE NOT SERIOUSLY GOING INTO AN ASTEROID FIELD?
IF I MIGHT REMIND YOU, CAPTAIN, THE PROBABILITY OF SUCCESSFULLY NAVIGATING SUCH AN OBSTACLE IS APPROXIMATELY 2,467 TO 1!

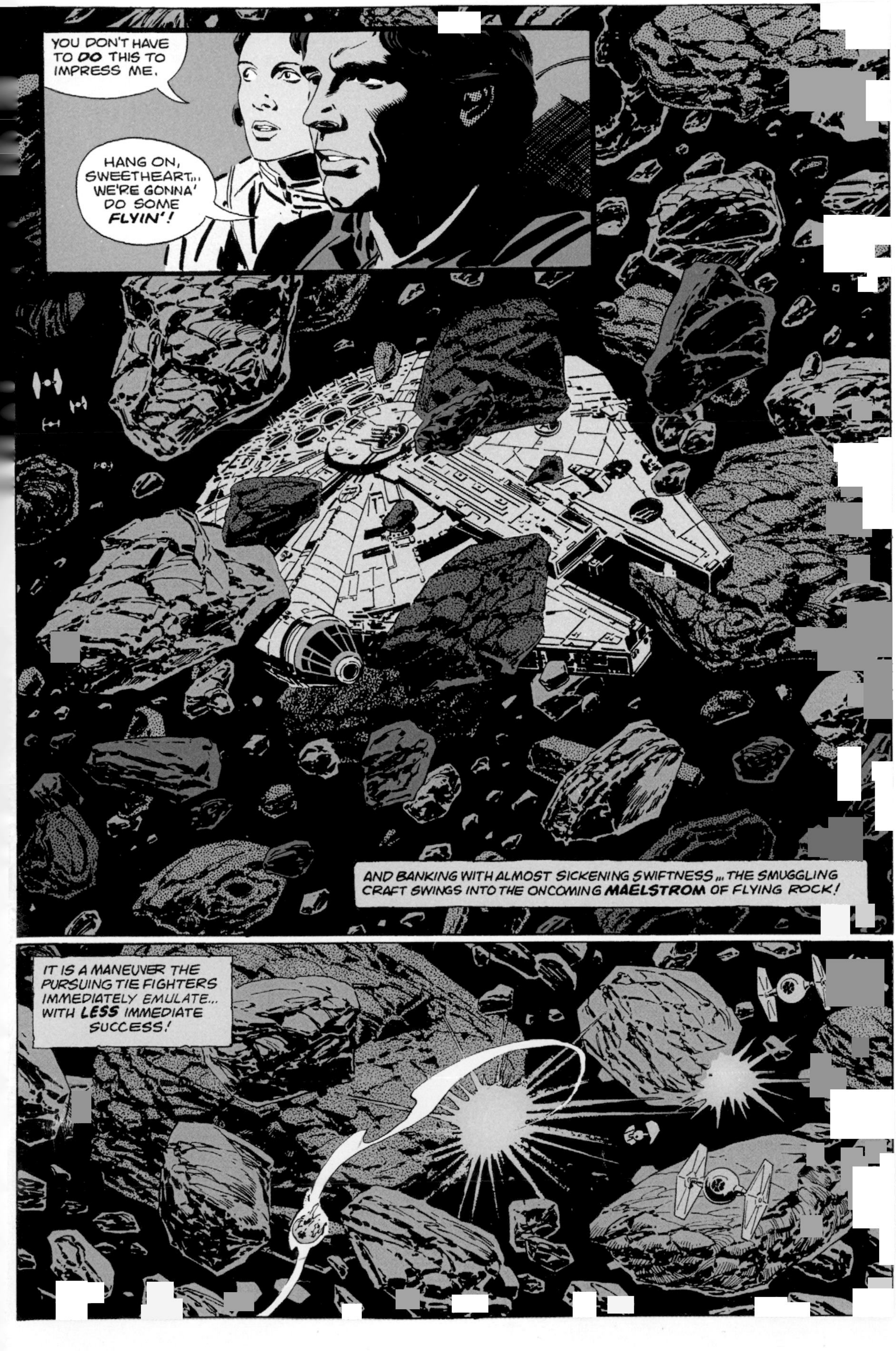
YOU DON'T HAVE TO DO THIS TO IMPRESS ME.
HANG ON, SWEETHEART... WE'RE GONNA' DO SOME FLYIN'!
AND BANKING WITH ALMOST SICKENING SWIFTNESS... THE SMUGGLING CRAFT SWINGS INTO THE ONCOMING MAELSTROM OF FLYING ROCK!
IT IS A MANEUVER THE PURSUING TIE FIGHTERS IMMEDIATELY EMULATE... WITH LESS IMMEDIATE SUCCESS!

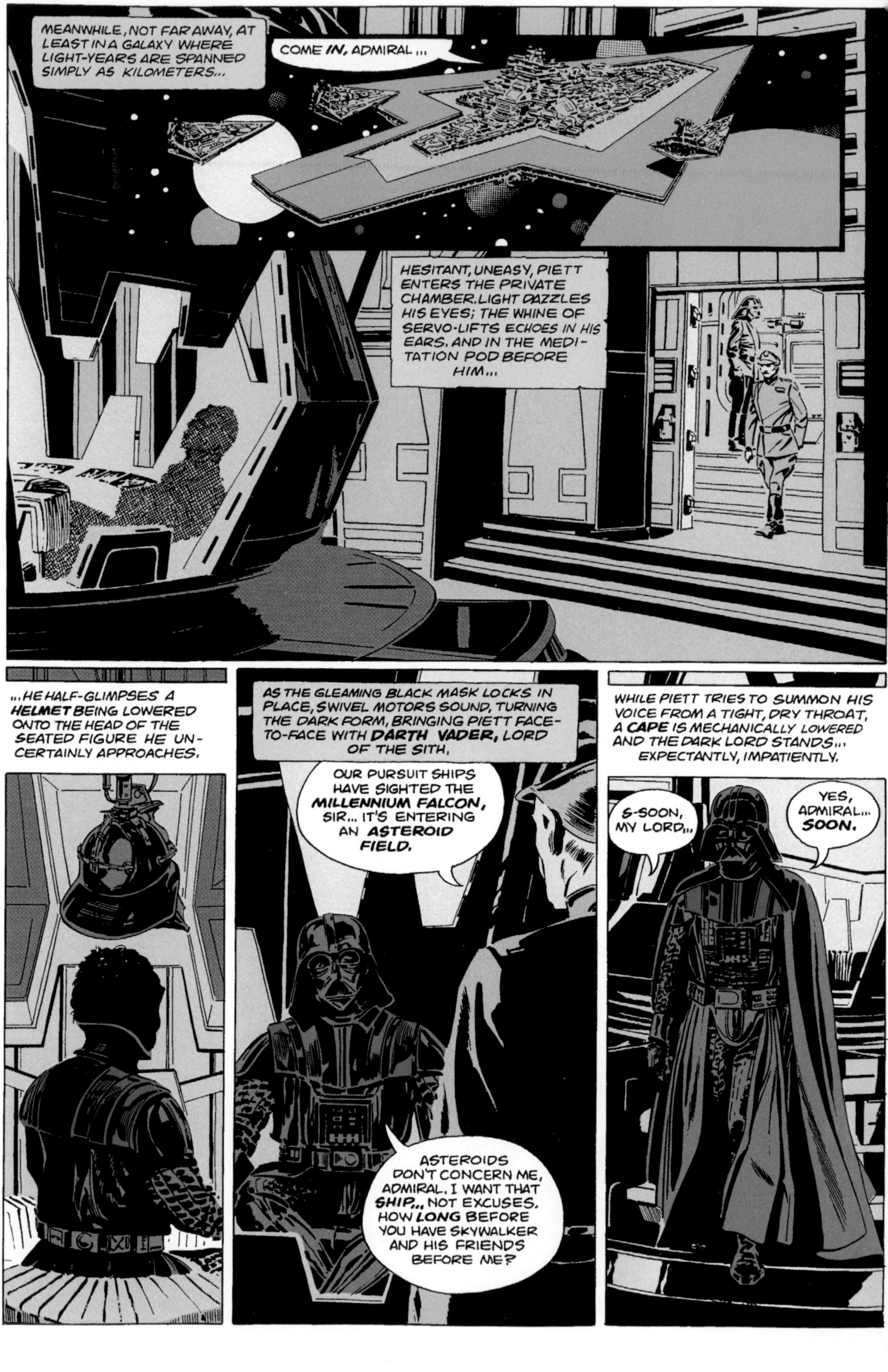
MEANWHILE, NOT FAR AWAY, AT LEAST IN A GALAXY WHERE LIGHT-YEARS ARE SPANNED SIMPLY AS KILOMETERS...
COME IN, ADMIRAL...
HESITANT, UNEASY, PIETT ENTERS THE PRIVATE CHAMBER. LIGHT DAZZLES HIS EYES; THE WHINE OF SERVO-LIFTS ECHOES IN HIS EARS. AND IN THE MEDITATION POD BEFORE HIM...
...HE HALF-GLIMPSES A HELMET BEING LOWERED ONTO THE HEAD OF THE SEATED FIGURE HE UNCERTAINLY APPROACHES.
AS THE GLEAMING BLACK MASK LOCKS IN PLACE, SWIVEL MOTORS SOUND, TURNING THE DARK FORM, BRINGING PIETT FACE-TO-FACE WITH DARTH VADER, LORD OF THE SITH.
OUR PURSUIT SHIPS HAVE SIGHTED THE MILLENNIUM FALCON, SIR... IT'S ENTERING AN ASTEROID FIELD.
ASTEROIDS DON'T CONCERN ME, ADMIRAL. I WANT THAT SHIP... NOT EXCUSES. HOW LONG BEFORE YOU HAVE SKYWALKER AND HIS FRIENDS BEFORE ME?
WHILE PIETT TRIES TO SUMMON HIS VOICE FROM A TIGHT, DRY THROAT, A CAPE IS MECHANICALLY LOWERED AND THE DARK LORD STANDS... EXPECTANTLY, IMPATIENTLY.
S-SOON, MY LORD...
YES, ADMIRAL... SOON.

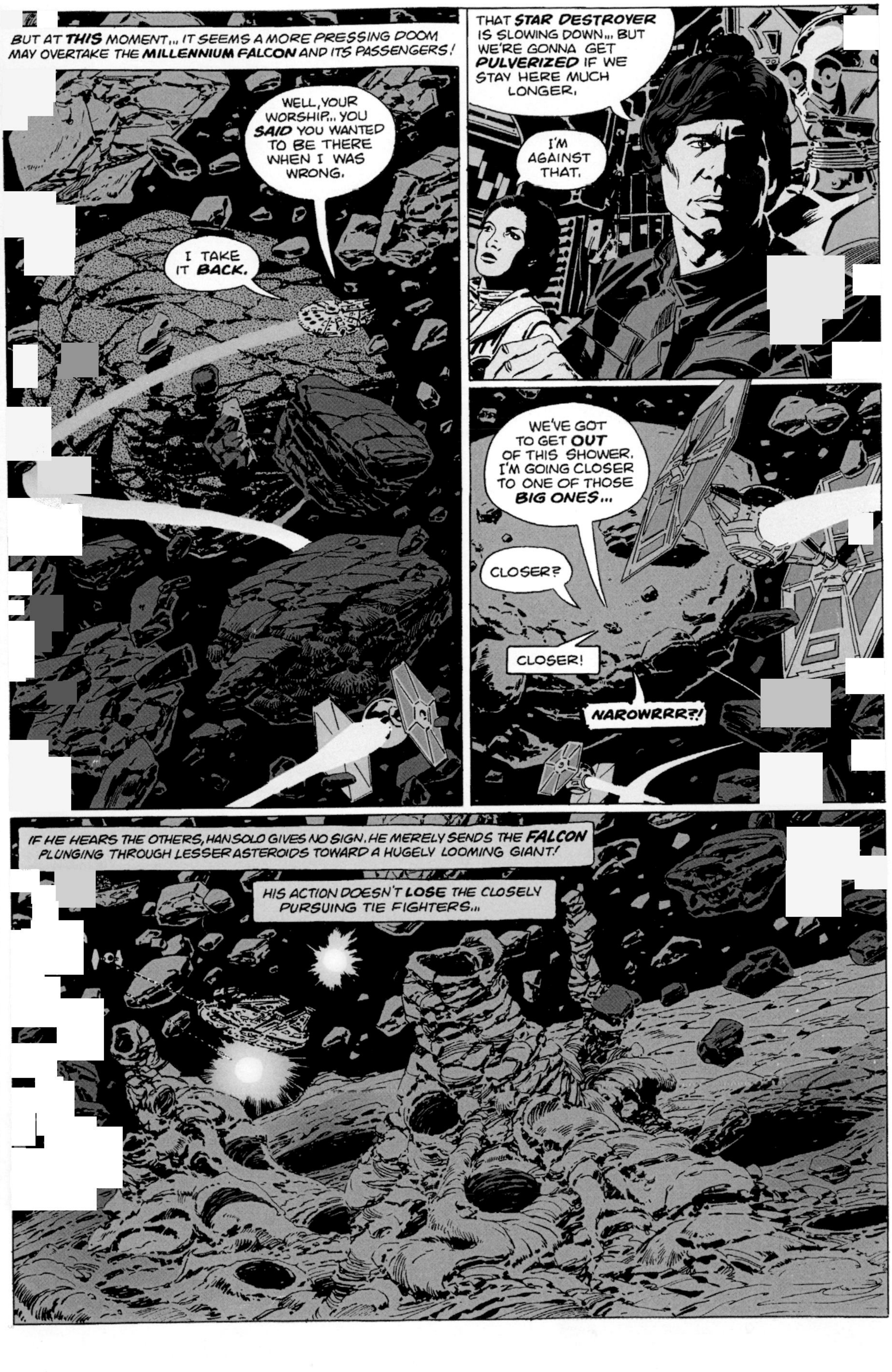
BUT AT THIS MOMENT... IT SEEMS A MORE PRESSING DOOM MAY OVERTAKE THE MILLENNIUM FALCON AND ITS PASSENGERS!
WELL, YOUR WORSHIP... YOU SAID YOU WANTED TO BE THERE WHEN I WAS WRONG.
I TAKE IT BACK.
THAT STAR DESTROYER IS SLOWING DOWN... BUT WE'RE GONNA GET PULVERIZED IF WE STAY HERE MUCH LONGER.
I'M AGAINST THAT.
WE'VE GOT TO GET OUT OF THIS SHOWER. I'M GOING CLOSER TO ONE OF THOSE BIG ONES...
CLOSER?
CLOSER!
NAROWRRR?!
IF HE HEARS THE OTHERS, HAN SOLO GIVES NO SIGN. HE MERELY SENDS THE FALCON PLUNGING THROUGH LESSER ASTEROIDS TOWARD A HUGELY LOOMING GIANT!
HIS ACTION DOESN'T LOSE THE CLOSELY PURSUING TIE FIGHTERS...

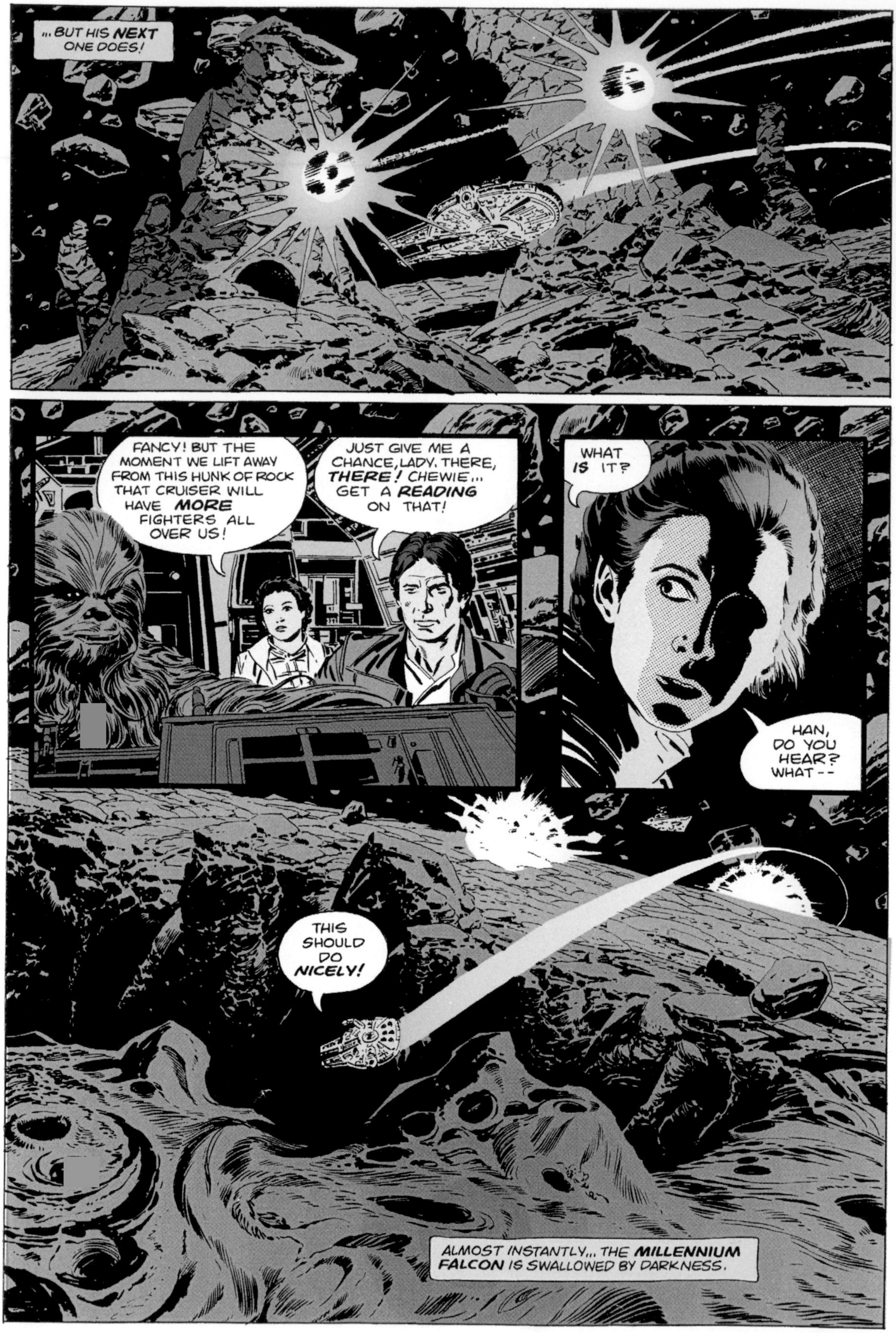

...BUT HIS NEXT ONE DOES!
FANCY! BUT THE MOMENT WE LIFT AWAY FROM THIS HUNK OF ROCK THAT CRUISER WILL HAVE MORE FIGHTERS ALL OVER US!
JUST GIVE ME A CHANCE, LADY. THERE, THERE! CHEWIE... GET A READING ON THAT!
WHAT IS IT?
HAN, DO YOU HEAR? WHAT --
THIS SHOULD DO NICELY!
ALMOST INSTANTLY... THE MILLENNIUM FALCON IS SWALLOWED BY DARKNESS.

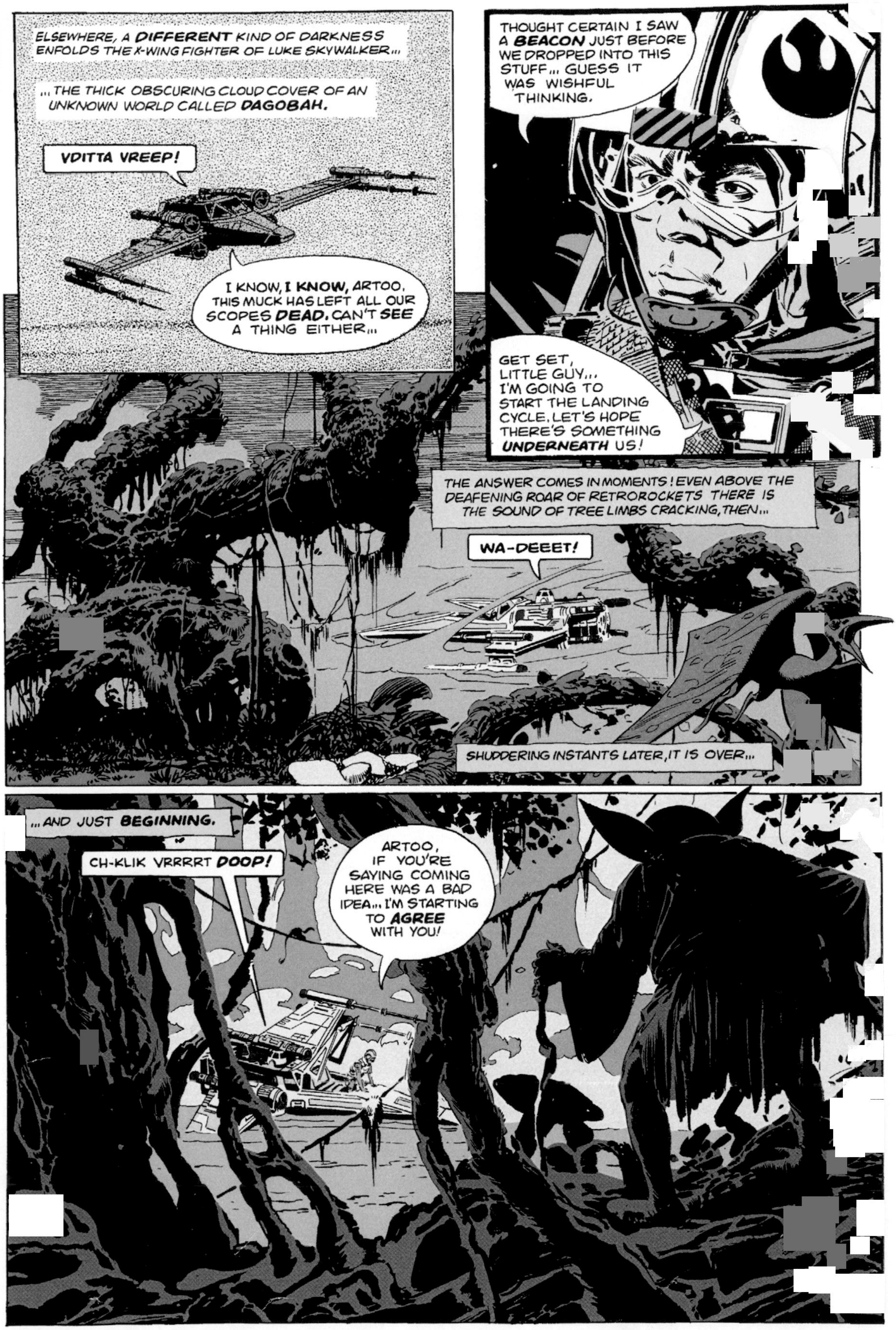
ELSEWHERE, A DIFFERENT KIND OF DARKNESS ENFOLDS THE X-WING FIGHTER OF LUKE SKYWALKER...
...THE THICK OBSCURING CLOUD COVER OF AN UNKNOWN WORLD CALLED DAGOBAH.
VDITTA VREEP!
I KNOW, I KNOW, ARTOO, THIS MUCK HAS LEFT ALL OUR SCOPES DEAD. CAN'T SEE A THING EITHER...
THOUGHT CERTAIN I SAW A BEACON JUST BEFORE WE DROPPED INTO THIS STUFF... GUESS IT WAS WISHFUL THINKING.
GET SET, LITTLE GUY... I'M GOING TO START THE LANDING CYCLE. LET'S HOPE THERE'S SOMETHING UNDERNEATH US!
THE ANSWER COMES IN MOMENTS! EVEN ABOVE THE DEAFENING ROAR OF RETROROCKETS THERE IS THE SOUND OF TREE LIMBS CRACKING, THEN...
WA-DEEET!
SHUDDERING INSTANTS LATER, IT IS OVER...
...AND JUST BEGINNING.
CH-KLIK VRRRRT DOOP!
ARTOO, IF YOU'RE SAYING COMING HERE WAS A BAD IDEA... I'M STARTING TO AGREE WITH YOU!

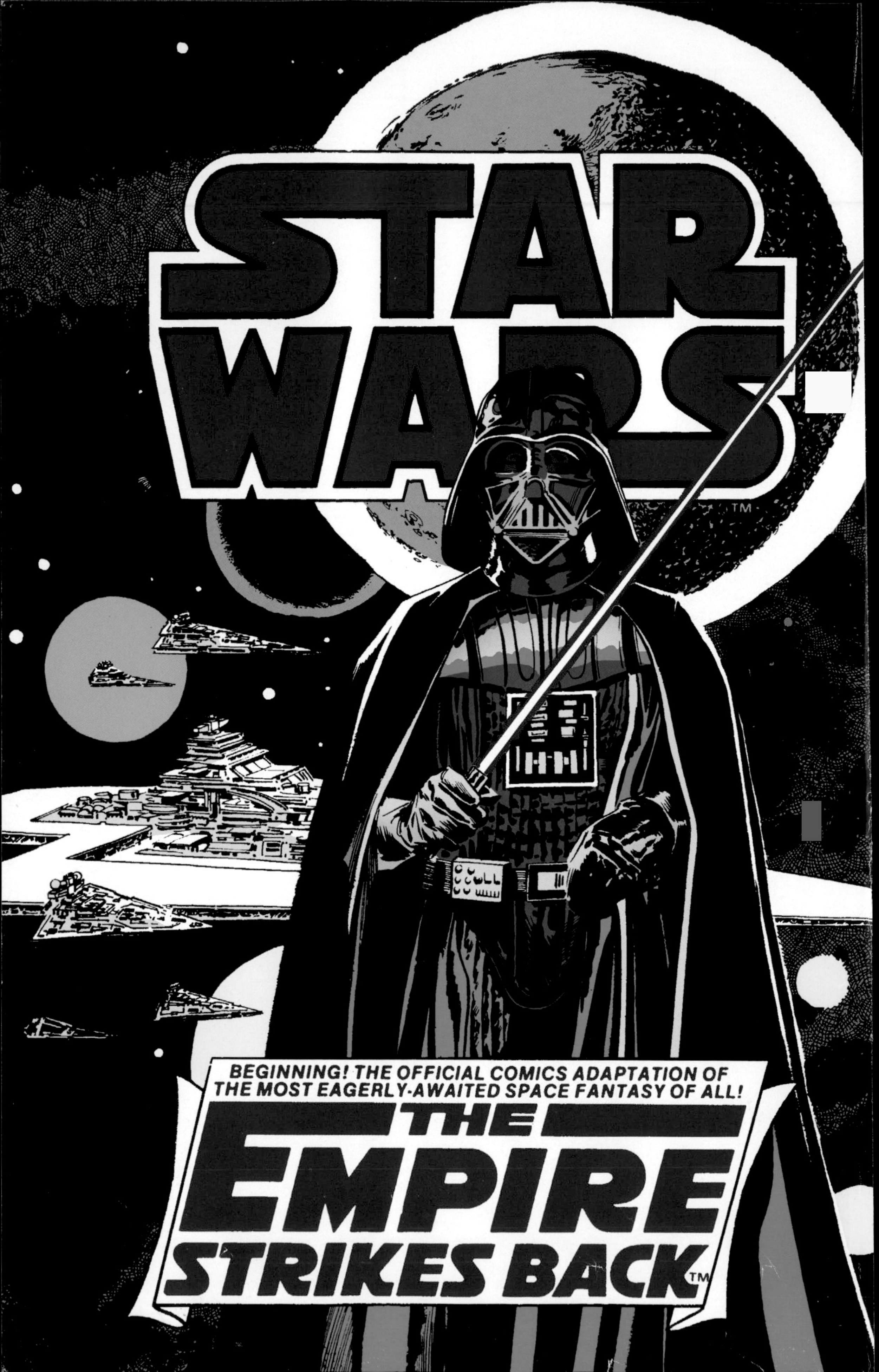
STAR WARS™
BEGINNING! THE OFFICIAL COMICS ADAPTATION OF THE MOST EAGERLY-AWAITED SPACE FANTASY OF ALL!
THE EMPIRE STRIKES BACK™